THE
DARK
WAR

THE DARK WAR

M. W. KOHLER

iUniverse LLC
Bloomington

The Dark War

iUniverse books may be ordered through booksellers or by contacting:

iUniverse LLC
1663 Liberty Drive
Bloomington, IN 47403
www.iuniverse.com
1-800-Authors (1-800-288-4677)

Because of the dynamic nature of the Internet, any web addresses or links contained in this book may have changed since publication and may no longer be valid. The views expressed in this work are solely those of the author and do not necessarily reflect the views of the publisher, and the publisher hereby disclaims any responsibility for them.

Any people depicted in stock imagery provided by Thinkstock are models, and such images are being used for illustrative purposes only.
Certain stock imagery © Thinkstock.

ISBN: 978-1-4917-0429-5 (sc)
ISBN: 978-1-4917-0430-1 (ebk)

Library of Congress Control Number: 2013915052

Printed in the United States of America

iUniverse rev. date: 08/21/2013

CONTENTS

Notes From The Author

This is the fourth book in *The Valley* series. With the defeat of Palakrine and the Dark Magic, the residents of all Domains celebrated. These celebrations lasted for a time, but then the parents began to be concerned about the pairings their children were making, and their ages. They all began to wonder, what will the descendants of the Keepers children and all of the descendents of the children of the Domains, of rightful magic face, as the years pass? There was one who wondered if the Dark Magic had truly been destroyed? Was there to be another threat? Could there be the need again, to face the horrors of Dark Magic and the evil minds that use it? Then, of course, there was the inevitable.

There is nothing in science or magic, that can stay the hands of the clock. It moves with the recklessness of youth and the cautiousness of age. It continues its relentless journey whether the hearts of those involved are pure, or tainted. As those of the Realm and the other Domains live, the clock lives with them. Neither will be stayed from their duties, or desires. As the peoples of the Domains live within the boundaries of time, the peace that follows Palakrine's defeat, brings an undeniable event, aging, and the results of it. Of course, we cannot forget the threat of the child of Palakrine, who was not slain as many thought, and, has created children of his own.

PROLOGUE

Saltakrine, son of Palakrine and nephew of Maltakrine, both previous rulers of the Dark Magic, and both failures at defeating the Overseer and the conquering of the Realm, surveyed the vast valley around him. He stood on a small rise to the southern side of the valley, dressed in the style of black clothes he had chosen as a young boy, a simple long sleeve shirt and trousers, and he looked to the two huge mountain ranges that protected the northern and southern borders of the land. He looked to the east and saw the funnel shaped, gradual incline of land that led to another mountain top and he knew that it too, would act as another barrier. He saw the many caves that dotted the cliffs to the southern side of that extended part of the valley, and he knew the Fire dragons would fare well in them. He looked to the river that wandered through this wide valley and emptied into the sea to the west and he knew those waters would also be a protective barrier and would be another food source for his people. He saw the huge forests, that would supply the logs necessary to build his city. He took a deep breath and smiled. He didn't turn as he spoke. "I have finally found it Starle! Begin transferring all here, as quickly as possible."

"Yes Master," Starle answered and whispered his spell, telling those who waited, to be ready. Shortly, a portal opened and the line of refugees began to parade from it.

"This will be our new home Starle," Saltakrine stated. "From here, I will do what that fool who sired me, and his brother could not. From here, I will take the Realm and much, much, more!" Starle grinned as he watched his master. Saltakrine could feel Starle's excitement and his smile grew. As he watched his people exit the portal, he thought of the many years he had struggled to get here.

Saltakrine could remember when his first true understanding of what he must do, had come to him. He had been very, very, young, just able to walk and not long after his father, Palakrine, had sent him to that isolated Domain. It was just prior to the assault on the Realm, that his father would lose. He remembered how he had felt the presence of the one who wanted his fathers, and his powers in the Dark Magic. Ponnope had been her name and greed had been her only purpose. He had looked into her eyes as she sent her spell of destruction at him. His defensive reactions saved his and Starle's life, but had not stopped the destruction of all around him. He had woken slowly, at first, and then the rage of Dark Magic came to him. He had no idea how much time had passed since he had seen Ponnope preparing to cast her spell to destroy him, but he remembered that he had been very hungry. He had learned later that it had been several days. He had opened his eyes and looked around. He finally had spotted the back of Starle's horned head through a opening in the collapsed timbers. "Starle!" he had called out and the head moved and then turned to him. Starle's reddened eyes looked to him and he smiled.

"Master, you live," Starle had cried. "I had not seen you moving and I feared I never would." Then the creatures eyes looked confused. "What happened?" he had asked. Saltakrine snarled with his memory.

"That bitch who thought herself my father's daughter, tried to kill us," he had told the son of a sorceress and a demon and he remembered the hatred and anger that had come with his words.

"Why would she do that?" Starle had asked, even more confused. Saltakrine smiled, in anger.

"Because she thought her valueless hide was worth more than ours and she wanted the power that was mine, for herself." Saltakrine remembered saying and looking around slowly. "Let us find a way out of this and find out what has happened since her failed efforts," he had said and started to wiggle towards a small light he could see. He had been surprised to see the small light begin to grow as hands moved dirt and debris and voices called for him.

"Do you think the Dark Lord has won?" Starle had asked as he too started to wiggle his way out.

"No," Saltakrine had said vehemently, as hands pulled him free from the would be tomb. He had stood and looked to the relieved faces of his rescuers. He remembered turning to Starle as a horrible grin had come to his lips. "Now we plan to do what Palakrine could not do!" Starle grinned back at him as the rescuers had looked from Saltakrine to Starle, confusion on their faces. "We will take the Realm for our own!" Saltakrine had announced and the others had cheered their new master!

Later in his life, older, but still young, he remembered looking around the dining room of the small castle that had been built, at the sorcerer's and sorceresses who ate at the table, seemingly lost in their own quiet conversations. He remembered looking to the food on his plate, almost half gone. He had realized that his hunger was not for food and he had risen from his chair at the head of the table. He had moved to and looked out of the window at the almost completely dead world his father had thought would only be a temporary home for him. "How could he have been so stupid?" he remembered asking the window, of his father. Neither the window, nor the land he could see through it, had given him an answer. His anger had tried to take him over and he had managed to fight it down. He had finally realized that he had the power to start looking for another home, where he could build the Domain he could see so clearly in his mind.

"Master?" Starle had asked quietly, from behind him. "You have not finished your food. Is there something wrong?"

"It is time to start looking for our new home Starle," Saltakrine had told him, and the sorcerer's and sorceresses, quietly. He had turned and left the room.

He had felt Starle, and the now silent sorcerer's and sorceresses still at the table, as they silently watched him leave, with worry in their eyes. Many years had passed before he had found this valley.

He now looked again to the valley that would hold his Dark City, and he smiled wider. *Yes,* he thought, *I will conquer the Realm and the Domains, and I will rule with the power of the Dark Magic!* His smile was quite wide as he walked to where his people, goblins, demons, and fire dragons had gathered. He quickly explained to all what he wanted and those assigned to the various jobs, began their work.

In the town of Zentler, as Saltakrine began the building of his Dark City, an awareness that would shake the peace of the Rightful Magic, began. "Miss Vicky, Miss Vicky!" Porsia called from the porch, her voice very excited. Vicky, wife of Willy, who was Mayor of the town of Zentler, turned and looked to her.

"What is it?" Vicky called from the garden, knowing that Porsia couldn't come to her because she was having so much trouble with her knees these days and couldn't handle the stairs.

"Master Cory and Miss Felicia have arrived and they have brought the young ones," Porsia called and Cory stepped from the door. Vicky's face lit up even brighter than

Porsia's, for it had been a long time since she had seen either of her children, or their families.

"I'm coming," she cried out, getting to her feet. She dropped the small shovel and her work gloves and tried to brush as much as the garden dirt from her as she could, as she raced for the porch. Cory laughed at the sight she made. Porsia had returned to the kitchen and as Vicky neared, she could hear the happy voices of reunion. As she neared the porch, she heard the knocker on the front door and then the ecstatic scream of joy and love from Porsia.

"Carmon, Tommy, children, oh how wonderful. Come in, come in," she cried out and Vicky could hear the tears of joy in her voice. Vicky dived into the open arms of her youngest and held on tight. He chuckled as he gently kissed her cheek.

"Hello mama," he said softly. She couldn't answer at first, for her tears of happiness.

"Oh my baby," was all she could finally squeak out. He chuckled as he held her.

"Is there room for another?" Felicia asked as she too came to the porch. Vicky did not even try to wipe her tears, or the gray hair from her face as she extended her arm and pulled the mother of her grandchildren into the embrace. It took a few moments and then Vicky had to speak.

"All I need is Cindy and this day would be the most perfect of days."

"Do you mean us?" Cindy asked as she, her husband George, and son, Marklen, sitting behind his father, rode into the yard. Vicky couldn't even speak as she looked to her daughter.

"At least we tied our horses out front, like normal people would," Cory told his older sister sarcastically and she laughed.

"Well, that means your horses will be breathing in the dust of the road and ours will not," Cindy told him with a grin as she hiked one leg over the saddle and slid from the horse. She ran up the steps and joined the widening group of huggers. George smiled and dismounted just in time to catch Marklen, as he jumped from the horse and raced for the porch, where the other children were gathering around their parents and their grandmothers. Porsia sat on the small bench that was part of the porch, her knees hurting, and watched the great hug and the tears of joy rolled down her cheeks. Carmon came to her and put her arms around her mother and shared her tears of joy. Marge, Tommy and Carmon's youngest, joined them by wiggling in between them and they both laughed at her. George and Tommy met at the bottom of the stairs and shared a handshake and a manly hug.

"Come on, let's get those horses off the road," George said. Tommy grinned and beckoned his oldest, Robert, who preferred Bob, to come with him and followed the much larger man around the house. As Bob came running around him, to be with the leader of the parade, Tommy had a powerful sensing. Grabbing his head and groaning loudly, he fell to his knees. His son had only just barely heard him and turned around and fear came to his very young eyes.

"Papa," he cried out and ran back to his father. George turned with the boys outcry and followed quickly.

"What is it Tommy?" George asked as he came and took Tommy's shoulders, pulling him back to his feet. Tommy looked to him with wide eyes.

"Get Cindy, I can't send right now," he told George in a hushed, hoarse voice, as he braced himself against the house. George nodded and ran around the building.

"Papa?" Bob asked with fear. Tommy looked to him and tried to smile.

"It will be alright son. Go get your mother, please," Tommy told the boy. Bob nodded and started to run around the building and nearly knocked his mother over as she led the family to Tommy. She came to her husband and took his arm, Carmon's eyes held fear for what her husband might have seen.

"What is it Tommy," Cindy asked as she stopped in front of him. He looked to her and there was fear in his eyes.

"Tell Heather and Zachia to come, Now!" he told her with a voice that had no volume, but great intensity. She didn't hesitate and within seconds, both Heather and Zachia stood in front of him. There was worry in their eyes and Tommy didn't give them a chance to ask. "I sensed the boy," he told them both, but he looked to

Zachia. "It was just a flash, but it was definitely the same boy, the son of Palakrine, and he is no longer a boy." Heather glanced at her brother, who had suddenly gone quiet to her. She trembled with the hard look that had come to his eyes.

"Are you absolutely sure?" Heather asked turning back to Tommy. Tommy's eyes were wide when he nodded slowly.

"Oh god, no," Carmon whispered, pulling both her children to her and leaning to her husband, as Heather called to her father, the Overseer. The others' closed to each other's arms as they thought of the horrible possibilities Tommy's words meant to all of the Domains.

Willy, who had been the youngest ever elected Mayor of the town of Zentler, at not yet eighteen, turned from his desk and watched the pigeon that had landed on his window sill. He had held the mayoral position now for many years. Through the door behind him, he could hear the loud voice of his secretary as she directed messengers, citizens, and would be sales people to the proper recipient for their attentions. He smiled softly for no reason he could understand. The news of the sensing Tommy had had years ago, died down with the passage of time, almost. He knew that most of the folk of magic had not forgotten. His son and daughter, as well as his grandchildren, showed the undercurrent of tension, almost constantly. Of course, now that Cory, Felicia and the kids had moved to the Valley, to assume the guidance of the Valley, after the deaths of Michael and Maria, and DeeDee and Tom, he didn't get see them as often as he would have liked, but he understood the need. There came a knock on the door and Mrs. Karbull stuck her head in. The rather pudgy woman, somewhere in her forties, whose hair was kept in a bun so tight that it pulled the skin of her face, and who sometimes took her position to a level it should not be, gave him a strained smiled.

"I'm sorry Mayor, but there's a young gentleman out here persistently saying you will see him, immediately," she told him with a certain amount of irritation in her voice.

"What's his name Mrs. Karbull?" Willy asked, turning from the pigeon, back to his desk.

"Uh, a Mr. Zachia, sir. Shall I schedule a appointment for him later sir?" she asked in her official voice. Willy smiled.

"No Mrs. Karbull, show him in and please make sure we are not disturbed, unless it's an emergency," Willy told her and the woman lifted her brows.

"Are you sure sir?" she asked with a thousand questions in her voice. He nodded at her and lost his smile.

"Yes Mrs. Karbull. Now, please," he told her and she slowly opened the door and stood aside as Zachia entered the office. The first thing Willy saw, was the intensity of Zachia's eyes.

"Shall I bring some coffee sir?" Mrs. Karbull asked as she watched the visitor take a chair and that he did not sit as a visitor to the Mayor should. Zachia had sat down, placing his elbows on his knees and clasping his hand together in front of him, looking to the floor. Willy saw the quick shake of Zachia's head and looked to his secretary, who was getting a very defensive look to her eyes.

"No thank you Mrs. Karbull. Please make sure we are not disturbed," Willy told her and met her eyes, waiting for her to leave. She glanced to him and then back to the visitor. "That will be all Mrs. Karbull," Willy told her, his voice going flat and official. She looked to him and she saw a look of irritation come to his eyes.

"Very well sir," she said and began to back from the room, pulling the door with her. She again looked to Zachia. *He's young, tall and well muscled, but I bet I can still throw him out on his ear*, she thought as she closed the door. Zachia looked to Willy and the intensity of his eyes had not lessened.

"Willy," Zachia started and Willy, knowing that the oldest son of the Overseer, would not be here if it were not something important, magically, held up his hand to stop him. Willy rose from his chair and went to the door. He slowly turned the knob and then yanked the door open. There, slightly bent over, was Mrs. Karbull, her ear planted to where the door had been. Willy kept his voice calm.

"Mrs. Karbull, why don't you get me the reports from the last three years inspections of the water system and also, make sure we are *not*, disturbed." Willy's voice had an angry edge to it with the last few words. Mrs. Karbull blushed at being caught, as she stood. She nodded and headed for the records room. Willy watched her until she turned the corner and then slowly closed the door again. He turned back to the son of his cousin, Mike, and returned to his desk. "Alright Zachia, what's on your mind?" he asked as he sat in his chair. Zachia didn't look up at first. He sat, his elbows still on his knees. His hands clasped before him. His fingers entwined, but the heels of his hands rubbed each other slowly. His eyes were burning a hole in the floor. Willy waited. Finally, Zachia's hands stopped moving and he lifted his eyes and looked to Willy as he straightened. Willy saw the same urgency, but also, a look of regret.

"I'm sorry, but I need to talk with Dremlivar," Zachia told him in a voice that was not loud, but very intense. Willy looked to him for a moment and then his right eye brow slowly lifted. Willy had become so accustom to the presence of Dremlivar, he had almost forgot that he was a separate entity, living within him.

"Why?" Willy asked cautiously. Zachia smiled, without smiling, his eyes locked on Willy's.

"I have to learn the basics of Dark Magic," he told his older cousin. "I have to learn what he had tried to teach Maltakrine." Willy stared at him for several minutes and then his eyes closed. When they opened, there was a look of concern and something Zachia had never seen before, the eyes of Dremlivar.

"What do you want to learn?" a strange voice asked, and Zachia knew he was talking with the old scholar of Contaria.

———⌁———

"Mensalon, can I talk with you?" Charlesia asked as she entered his office at the mines.

"What is it my wife?" Mensalon, son of Phemlon and Remlic asked, standing and turning to her. She came to him and kissed him gently.

"I'm worried about Morsalon," she told him as they sat on the couch. He looked to her strangely.

"What about him?" Mensalon asked cautiously about their son. "Has he done something wrong?" She glanced at him and then looked to her hands.

"Not so much wrong, as different. Different enough to cause me worry," she said softly. He waited. "I know that sometimes, elfin children can play roughly, but when we went to visit the palace the other day, Morsalon was what we call, malicious. He would lay in wait and cause the other children pain and he would smile when they would cry out." She glanced at him again, then to her hands. "It was Pelidora that brought it to my attention." He looked to her a moment and then he looked to her hands and saw that she was wringing them. "I went and watched the children play for awhile and saw that the other children didn't want to play with him. They would try to run from him," she added softly. "Then I saw what Pelidora was talking about. He intentionally pinched Ventia and laughed when she cried. I stopped him and took him with me the dining room where all the parents had been talking and made him sit with me and he glared at me the entire time, and muttered." Charlesia looked to him and there was tears starting. "Later, Pelidora told me she was getting a very wrong sensing of him. A Dark Magic sensing's!" Mensalon looked to her, his eyes wide.

"There has never been a elf with Dark Magic before. How could she be sensing that? She must be wrong," he stated and stood, looking at her. She stood as well and looked to him.

"I was going to take him to your father and find out his opinion. I wanted you to know before I did it though," she told him. He stared at her for a moment.

"I will go with you and we will see if Pelidora has had a true sensing," he told her and they left for their home. They had only just arrived and were talking with their Wingless nanny, when there came a knock on the door. Mensalon went and opened it and then stood aside as Patoria charged in and went straight for Morsalon's room. Charlesia and Mensalon exchanged looks, for they both knew that Patoria was an elder with the strongest ability to sense Dark Magic! Four Guardians were right behind her and Mensalon and his father Phemlon, followed behind them. Remlic, Mensalon's mother, went to Charlesia and put her arm around her shoulders.

"Patoria came to Phemlon, at our home, and told him that she was feeling a very faint sensing of Dark Magic. Phemlon summoned the Guardians and we followed her here," Remlic told Charlesia. The oldest child of Megan began to cry as she tried to tell Remlic of the events at the palace. Remlic pulled the girl into her arms.

"There has never been an elf with Dark Magic before," she whispered, more to herself than Charlesia. Charlesia cried harder as she thought that she was the reason for this. What was she do about the one who was beginning to grow within her now? They both heard Morsalon cry out and a lot of tussling. Finally, they all came from the room, except Morsalon. Mensalon came to his wife and took her from his mother and held her. Remlic went to Phemlon and into his arms, whispering what Charlesia had told her. Patoria stood at the door of Morsalon's room, watching the boy, who was now under a gentle sleep spell. Charlesia started to calm with Mensalon's whispered words and finally calmed enough to sit by herself. Patoria came to her, pulling another chair with her. She sat down facing Charlesia and took her hands into hers and looked into the tear reddened eyes of the young mother.

"I think that because the boy is only half elf, that the whisper of Dark Magic that holds him, was able to take root. I have placed an amulet on him that will halt the growth of it within him and hopefully, pull it from him. It is all we can do at this time. The Dark Magic is very weak and there is hope that this will work." Patoria tried to smile at Charlesia. The young mother looked to her and then to Mensalon. Returning her eyes to the elder elf, she began to cry again.

"I'm pregnant again," she whispered between sobs. Absolute silence followed her words.

It was years later when Charlesia again faced Patoria. "The amulet is not working Patoria." Charlesia told the elder. The elf looked to her and then she looked to the wall, frowning.

"I was afraid of this," Patoria said. "Especially since Belanor was born." Charlesia looked at her confused.

"Why would that matter? She has no Dark Magic, you have been checking her. How can that be an effect with Morsalon?" Charlesia asked, her heart sinking that she had somehow caused this problem too. The elf turned and came to her.

"It is not what Belanor has or has not done that is the problem. It is the way Mensalon treats Morsalon since the girl was been born," Patoria told her. Charlesia looked to her still confused. Patoria smiled softly. "Morsalon is being pushed from his father, by his father's lack of attention," Patoria said. "That is breeding resentment and this brings his emotions to a higher peak. Those heightened emotions are over powering the amulet and allowing the Darkness within Morsalon to grow and feed on his pain and anger."

"What am I to do?" the young mother asked, her fear very clear in her voice. Patoria placed her hands on both of her arms.

"You must convince Mensalon to give the attention the boy needs and wants or, I am afraid you will lose Morsalon to the Dark Magic," the elf was all but whispering the last words. Charlesia nodded and hurried home. When she neared her home, she heard the angry sounds of her son and husband. She hurried on and then there was a crash. The door exploded open and Morsalon fled the house, shoving her from his way and throwing the amulet Patoria had placed on him, that he had never been able to remove before, away.

"Morsalon, wait," she cried out as he ran east and disappeared into the trees of the forest. She looked into the house and saw Mensalon laying on the floor, blood coming from a gash on his head and Belanor was using a rag to try and stop the bleeding. She hurried into the house and took the rag from her daughter. "Get a bowl with some water in it and some more rags," she told the girl as gently as she could and tended her husband. Later, after getting Mensalon to bed and comfortable, Charlesia asked Belanor what had happened. The girl hesitated. "Tell me Belanor, please." The girl looked to her and then to her father, tears of not understanding coming to her eyes.

"Morsalon came from his room, screaming at papa. He made no sense, just ranting. When papa tried to calm him, Morsalon grabbed up a chair to hit papa and ran out." Belanor started to cry. Charlesia took her daughter into her arms and called to Heather for help. Heather told Mike, and he gathered Morgan, Natoria and Megan. They brought a healer and Mensalon would recover. Morsalon was looked for, but was not found.

The hands of the clock continued their march and then; Saltakrine stood, looking from the balcony of the fortress and smiled. As soon as his son, Balakrine, born of a sorceress, had reached maturity, he had started mating him to sorceresses and the third child of those couplings had just been delivered. He finally had a girl, born by the most powerful of Dark Magic, to begin building his army of Dark Magic sorcerers. One of the hardest things that Saltakrine had been forced to accept was that although Balakrine was slightly more powerful in Dark Magic than he, his ability to think ahead, or even quickly was severely hampered. Balakrine was suddenly standing beside him. Saltakrine looked to the boy with a grin. Balakrine smiled back.

"You have a girl now, to begin building your army," Balakrine said. "When can we begin?" Saltakrine smiled, trying to hide his worry about the boy.

"We have to wait until she can breed son," Saltakrine told him with a quiet chuckle; "but with luck, you will breed another and that will add to our reserves." The boy laughed.

"I'll do my best," he said and they both laughed.

"Good, I'll send another sorceress to you tonight!" Saltakrine said and slapped the boys back. Balakrine grinned widely. Unfortunately, the boy could never created another girl and this did not please his father.

―――⁕――――

Mike was going over the reports from the different Domains when Heather appeared in his office. Mike actually jumped from the sudden appearance.

"Honey, you might want to announce yourself before you do that. I'm getting on in years and surprises like that can be dangerous for someone my age," he chuckled when he said it and saw that Heather was not smiling. He frowned. "What's the matter honey?" She looked to him and the worry was very clear in her eyes. She came around the desk and rested her backside against the desk, beside Mike's chair. She looked at him and shrugged, just slightly.

"I'm not sure, but Zachia's not opening his mind to me completely. Hasn't been for several years now, and Sen told me the other day, that he's been doing some pretty strange things with his powers." Mike waited and Heather seemed stalled.

"What things honey?" Mike finally asked. Heather looked to him.

"I don't know," she told him and took a shaky breath. "Normally, when he used his magic, I could feel it, but I haven't felt anything but the usual, minor things, for years." She looked to him. "I think Zachia has learned a new kind of magic and he's hiding it from me, and everyone else." Mike smiled at his daughter.

"Honey, there's only two kinds of magic. The Rightful Magic and the Dark Magic," Mike told her and she nodded, looking to him, slowly lifting her brows.

"I know daddy," she said softly. "If what Sen has told me is the truth, I think Zachia is dabbling in Dark Magic." Mike stared at his daughter for some time before he answered her.

"That's a very serious charge Heather. Do you have any proof?" he asked, trying to keep his voice calm. She shook her head and looked to her hands as she pretended to clean her nails.

"Nothing definite, just a lot of things that don't add up," she said and glanced at her father and then back to her hands, that she was now slowly rubbing together.

"Like what things?" Mike urged her. She sighed.

"Ever since Tommy had his sensing of Palakrine's son, he has been different," Heather told him. Mike nodded.

"You told me about his shutting off from you and the look in his eyes, but that was a long time ago," Mike said, urging her to say more. She nodded and looked to the wall she faced.

"He's never opened back up to me completely since. He has been possessed in finding the one Tommy sensed. He's had Tommy and many of the other seers, Pielsakor, Dorence and others', searching for Saltakrine constantly," Heather said softly. Mike nodded and waited. "He had spent a lot of time working with his children, Renoria and Zandian, on their magical talents and suddenly all but quit working with them and started to work with Ventia and she's changed as well. Not much, but Chrystal says the girl is much more serious about everything." Heather took a deep breath and Mike waited for more. "I've been talking with Sen and she told me that five years ago, Zachia spent several months visiting Zentler regularly, with Willy." Mike lifted his brows slightly.

"Why would he do that?" Mike wondered more than said. Heather nodded and looked to her father.

"That's what I've come to ask you to find out. Daddy, I'm scared. I don't like what Zachia is becoming. He has never hidden from me like this before and I'm scared!" She didn't even try to stop the tears as they started down her cheeks. Mike stood and took her into his arms. He held her as she cried and his mind raced. He did not like what he was thinking.

"Mike!" Vicky stated in surprise when she had answered the knocking of the door. She quickly gave him a family hug. He returned the hug and pulled from her showing a strained smile. She sobered instantly.

"What's wrong now?" she asked, in almost a whisper, her eyes showing her concern.

"Is Willy around? I tried at town hall, but it seems it's closed today," he asked and said and a smile toyed with Vicky's mouth.

"It's Sunday Mike," she said. "Come in, Willy's in the back yard." Mike nodded and Vicky led the way through the house and out the back door.

"Willy," Vicky called out; "Mike's here to see you." Willy looked up and Mike thought he saw a flicker of some kind in his cousin's eyes. Willy rose from his chair and approached. When he got close, he looked at Mike.

"Is my office alright?" he asked. Mike nodded, accepting a glass of lemonade from Vicky with thanks. Vicky watched as the two went into the house and she was worried about her husband's sudden serious attitude.

"Have a seat," Willy said as he closed the door behind him. Mike sat in the chair in front of the desk. Willy went to the rear of the desk and got the carat of brandy and two small snifters from a cabinet. He turned and looked at the glass in Mike's hand. "Do you want it with the lemonade or separate?" Mike smiled and set the glass down.

"Separate, please," he said.

"This is about Zachia, right?" Willy asked as he sat and poured the brandy, handing Mike his. Mike nodded and brought the snifter to his mouth for the first sip.

"What happened?" Mike asked after his sip and he had set the snifter on the desk. "Did Zachia talk with Dremlivar?" Willy nodded as he set his snifter down. "What about?" Mike asked managing to keep his voice calm. Willy looked to him.

"He wanted to know the basics of Dark Magic, what Dremlivar had tried to teach Maltakrine." Mike's brows lifted and Willy put up his hand. "Not how to use Dark Magic, but what made it work. How to use that knowledge to find one who controls Dark Magic." Willy took another sip of brandy. Mike copied him as he thought.

"Heather and his wife Senfarna, are worried that ever since Tommy's sensing, Zachia has become possessed in finding the son of Palakrine, and that he is now actually using Dark Magic to do so, and, I'm not sure he isn't," Mike said softly. Willy looked at him.

"Really?" he asked quietly. He picked up the snifter and drained it. He quickly refilled it and set the glass on the desk. "With his power," a different, vaguely familiar voice caused Mike to look up suddenly; "he should have been more than capable to resist the effect." Mike looked to the eyes of Dremlivar. "Are you sure he's using Dark Magic?" Mike shook his head and drained the snifter he had picked up. He held it out and Dremlivar refilled it.

"No, I'm not, but Heather is pretty well convinced that he is and she closer to him than any other." Dremlivar nodded.

"Talk to your son Mike, with an elf or two close by." Dremlivar told him. "That should tell you all you need to know." Mike nodded and drained the glass again.

"That's pretty much what I was going to do." Mike started to get up and then stopped, looking to Dremlivar. "Did you say how to find a user of Dark Magic by using Dark Magic to do it?" Dremlivar smiled and shook his head.

"Knowing the makeup of Dark Magic does not mean using it. But, with the knowledge of how Dark Magic works, someone with rightful magic, can locate a user of Dark Magic." Mike looked at him for a moment.

"That means he could have just been searching, not using it," Mike said more to himself than to Dremlivar. The one behind the desk nodded, a slight grin on his face. Mike smiled. "Thank you Dremlivar, thank you." Willy smiled back at him.

"You're welcome cousin. Say hello to Gloreana for me." Mike nodded and disappeared. The sands of time flowed, unchecked.

"Zachia, No!" Gloreana screamed out as she sat up in bed. Mike came up with her and took her into his arms.

"What is it Gloreana," Mike called to her. She looked at him and tears over filled her panicked eyes and flooded her cheeks.

"Zachia goes to his death!" she screamed and fainted.

In another part of the palace, Sen lay listening to the sounds of Zachia's breathing and she knew he did not sleep. Suddenly his breathing stopped. She waited as panic began to fill her. She started to turn to him when he suddenly sat up. "I've found you," he hissed and threw the blanket from him and grabbed for his clothes.

"Zachia, what is it? What are you doing?" Her voice told of her building panic. He turned to her, his eyes wide with hatred, and desire. She felt true fear as she looked into his eyes.

"I've found him!" he screamed at her and disappeared. She stared at the vacant air, unable to erase the look she had seen in his eyes. She called to Heather, just after Heather had woken with her own horrifying seeing.

"What's the matter Sen?" Heather asked in a voice that held the truth of her own fears. "He's gone?" she asked, all but screaming.

"Yes," the panic could not be taken from Sen's thoughts. "He screamed he had found him and disappeared. Oh Heather, what am I to do?"

"I'll contact daddy and Tommy. Maybe we can track him. Hold on Sen, hold on!" Heather called to her father. She searched as she called and at first, she could feel his closure to her.

"Can you track him?" Mike asked her as soon as she called."

No daddy. I could feel him at first, but he's closed from me completely and I have no idea where he is. I'm calling Tommy and anybody else I can think of," she said and broke off from him. Mike, still sitting in bed, looked to his wife. The mother who just screamed her seeing of their son's death, and had fainted from the horror of that seeing, and who now lay in his arms. He wept with the breaking of his heart. Those of all Domains quickly began to appear in the entrance hall of the palace, many still in their bed clothes. Mike got Pelidora, who had come running into the room with Gloreana's screams, to care for Gloreana and joined the gathering in the entrance hall

In a fortress far from the Realm, Zachia appeared in the strange entrance hall and immediately went to a defensive stance. His heart raced as he looked around the darkness.

"Well, well," a voice came from somewhere, echoing through the hall. "What brings the Overseer's son to my Domain and, alone?" the voice asked maliciously.

Tommy had strained to find Zachia. He struggled to keep calm as he frantically searched with all of his talent. Finally, he called to Heather, in the Realm. "I've got him, but I don't know where he is and he is not alone," Tommy told Heather and the gathered, for Heather was passing on his words. "There are two of them and Zachia fights alone." The people in the entrance hall of the palace, listened with their minds to what Heather fed them.

Laughter, in a higher pitch, echoed through the dark. Zachia realized that he now faced two. "I have come to finish the job your sister failed to do Saltakrine!" Zachia called out.

"Is that right son of the Overseer?" Saltakrine asked from somewhere. "And how do you plan to beat me, and, my son?" Zachia remembered all that Dremlivar had taught him and closed his eyes. He opened his senses and let them guide him. "Why do you not answer Zachia? Oh yes, I know your name. Do you now realize the stupidity you have preformed?" Zachia threw up a hand and cast a powerful blast spell where his senses told him Saltakrine was. "Damn!" Saltakrine cried out, barely getting his shield up in time, but he couldn't stop the collapse of the section of the balcony, when the pillar he had been hiding behind was blown apart from Zachia's blast spell. He just did manage to get out from under most of it, except for his right foot. He screamed out as the huge log crushed his foot. Zachia cast two more powerful spells at the sound, each doing more damage than he thought they would. Then he sensed the other one, just passed the one he had killed. He raised his shield just in time for the blast spell to break harmlessly against it. He cast another spell and was rewarded with a pained outcry. He waited, listening, as silence closed in around him.

"They battle," Tommy cried out. "Zachia has destroyed Saltakrine but the other attacks." Tommy's voice held the horror of what his senses were telling him. "Zachia has beaten them!" Tommy screamed out and those words echoed through all the minds Heather was feeding. Every one of those minds cheered. Tommy had to scream to be heard over them. "Wait, wait, there is another, of greater power!" he screamed to them. "Zachia has lowered his defenses, not knowing of the third one!"

Zachia opened his eyes and started towards the ones he knew he had beaten. This time he was going to make sure that the evil was destroyed! With his concentration on the ones he had battled, he did not sense the blast spell launched at him from the balcony that surrounded the hall, by two small hands that controlled even more power than Saltakrine, or his son. When he did sense its approach, it was too late.

Heather screamed out, lunging to her father, who caught her and pulled her into his arms. Mike held his daughter tightly as she sobbed. His eyes traveled around the room and all wept at what seemed to be the truth. When Mike's eyes reached the bottom of the stairs, he looked into the red, tear swollen eyes of Gloreana.

"Daddy," Heathers sobbing, muffled voice came to all ears; "Zachia is gone." Mike closed his eyes, concentrating. Suddenly, the twisted body of Zachia appeared on the floor before him. Gloreana and Sen both screamed and fell upon the body of son and husband. The only sounds were the sobbing of all there. They could not hear the other sobbing, in every Domain. It would be many years after, Heather would tell all, that even held in Tyrus's arms, she never felt so alone, not having the one with her that had always been a part of her. Time continued its relentless journey.

Relkraen, lead Meleret of the palace, came into the dining room, during lunch, and whispered something in Mike's ear. Mike turned and looked to him, his eyes wide.

"What?" he asked much louder than he should have, which caused all those at the table to quiet and look to him in surprise. Relkraen shrugged and nodded. "I'll be right back," Mike announced to the room angrily, throwing his napkin at his plate as he stood. He walked from the room with a frown on his face. They all turned to Relkraen who smiled nervously, shrugged and hastily retreated to the kitchen. Gloreana watched the Meleret leave. She then rose and looked around the table.

"Everybody, finish your meals. I'll find out what's going on," she told them all and followed her husband. There were many confused and concerned looks exchanged by those still at the table. She walked into Mike's office and heard his words as he spoke into the orb.

"I am honored to meet you both, King Cranedoran and Queen Xanaloren, but I must ask, why have we not heard from you before this?" There was a slightly higher than normal toned voice that replied.

"We are sorry Lord Overseer, but until we were sure that you could again defeat the powers of the Dark Magic, we had chosen to keep ourselves hidden," the voice said as Gloreana walked to Mike's side. The two who could be seen in the orb, turned their eyes to her.

"Allow me to present my wife, Gloreana," Mike told the two strangers. "Gloreana, the King and Queen of Corsendora, King Cranedoran and Queen Xanaloren." As they were named, the two in the orb bowed, the Queen smiling with her bow. Gloreana returned their bows.

"It is an honor to meet you both, your Majesties," Gloreana said calmly and glanced to Mike.

"Perhaps Lord Overseer," King Cranedoran said; "it would be possible for us to visit the Realm and explain our decisions to you personally?" The King looked a little uncomfortable with the rest of his words. "The two prince's, our sons, think that it would be beneficial to both Domains, although they thought that we should have done this before the battle." He all but whispered the last. Mike quickly glanced at Gloreana and then back to the King.

"I think that would be fine your majesty. Say tomorrow, after the sun has reached high?" Mike said and asked. The King and Queen both nodded.

"Until tomorrow then," King Cranedoran stated and broke the connection.

"What was that all about?" Gloreana asked, rather loudly.

"It would seem that there is another Domain, that chose to sit out the battles and then, make peace with the victor!" Mike stated and there was no happiness in his voice. "Well, we better start letting everyone know," Mike said as he turned to return to the dining room. "I just hope nobody decides to over react to this," he added.

"You mean like you are now?" Gloreana whispered, wearing a worried grin, as she followed him. Mike nodded without turning his head.

———⁓⬦◦⬦◦⬦◦⬦⁓———

Word of the coming meeting with the newly discovered King and Queen was spread quickly. As per the Overseers instructions, most began to arrive long before lunch was served. Semitor and his family, arrived with a new member, Ralitor. He had been Solitor's best friend, and had taken over the responsibility of seeing to the needs of Pilsekor and her son, which was the custom when the brother could not. During that time, he and Pilsekor had become very close.

All the Domains were represented and all were very upset that this Domain had not joined in the battle against the Dark Magic. Lunch was a loud meal for them all, as they discussed the what's and why's. All during the meal, Gloreana could not help but notice Mike's calm and quiet attitude, when yesterday, he had been so angry. She also could not help but notice the slightest of a belly bump on her oldest daughter, indicating that she and Tyrus had probably rushed their wedding night, slightly. In fact, as she looked around the room, all of the older girls, recently wed, were showing results of the hasty efforts in the privileges of their marriages. As the meal ended and Melerets and the other servants cleared the table, the Domain leaders and their families, moved to the Reception room, where the expected guests were to be met.

Mike tried to keep his voice calm as he talked with each of them and Gloreana was with him constantly, for she sensed something in him that worried her. A feeling of hidden anger. Even Heather and Tyrus stayed near, for Heather sensed the same thing in her father. It took some time, but Mike was finally able to bring a simple calm to the group. The main thought that he told them was, that until they knew the true reasons, it would be wrong to jump to conclusions about this Domains actions. It was during the time of heads being nodded to the sense of Mike's words, that a Guardian announced the opening of a portal, outside of the gate. Mike signaled that the guests were to be shown in and a strange quiet settled over the gathered.

They entered with a calmness of walk that challenged the smoothness and grace of a Wingless. They each were dressed all in white. Each with a high collar, trimmed in gold, that started as any other collar in front, but rose to a pointed height behind their heads. Everyone immediately saw that none wore a crown of any kind, though the Queen did have several gold pins in her beautifully fashioned hair. The shining gold braiding on the shoulders, and buttons on the Kings and Prince's coats, dazzled the eyes, though there were a few men that thought the gold stripes that ran the length of their pants leg, was a bit much. The beautifully designed gold trimmings of the Queens lavish, long gown, caused most of the women present to feel envy. They all were tall, thin of build and tanned lightly, with light colored hair. Both King and Queen were surprised by the number that awaited them, and the sudden fascination of their two sons for the daughters of Keepers of Magic for the North East / South West Domains, and Dolaris, as the two young women had said, rather loudly, *Oh Yeah*, when they had seen the two princes. The King and Queen quickly regained their composer and faced The Overseer.

"Lord Overseer," the King began. "I am honored that you have agreed to this meeting, though, I had not expected this great a gathering." The King bowed, placing a restraining hand on the shoulder of the rather tall young man beside him, for the boy had taken a step towards Maelie, grinning. "May I present my wife, Queen Xanaloren," indicating her with his right hand; "and my children. To my left, our oldest son, Prince Crendosa and to the right of my Queen, our youngest son, Prince Crondasa." The Queen had also placed a restraining hand the Prince beside her, for the boy had started to walk towards Brei, grinning widely. "I am King Cranedoran, of the Domain Corsendora and I have come to explain," here the king hesitated slightly as his eyes swept the room; "our position of waiting." Mike and the others of the room had all bowed with the introductions, but every eye in the room was on them now, and not all were friendly.

Katie and Wistoria had to each place a hand of restraint on their daughters, who seemed quite willing to meet the Prince's halfway or even where they were. Brei slowly, but firmly, removed her mother's hand, but held her place and there was a determined look in the girls eyes that worried Katie. She glanced to Jarpon and was irritated that he had not seen their daughters actions. Then, as she looked to him, the memory of her own reactions when she had first seen him came back to her and she looked to her daughter with more understanding, until Dana leaned close and whispered to her.

"You did not give birth to a shy girl with her, mama," her oldest told her and Katie's heart took a jump.

"Oh shit," she whispered and looked to Brei, who had not taken her eyes from the young Prince Crondasa.

———

"I am sure that all of you are wondering why we did not join in the war with the Dark Forces, and I know that many of you are angered that we did not," King Cranedoran said to the representatives of the Domains and there were several heads that nodded. The King saw those nods and almost smiled. "Let me begin my explanation by saying that there has not been a war, of any kind, on Corsendora, in any of our history." Silence and wary expressions answered his statement. "We stayed separated from this war, simply because we do not know how to fight one." The silence of the room was now joined by the wide eyes of the listeners. "The people of Corsendora have always been a peaceful people. The thought of fighting repulses, and terrifies us." Looks of concern were now exchanged with looks of condemnation. "Then came the births of our sons and the thousands of other children, throughout the Domain of Corsendora and almost every one came to us, with the acceptance of fighting as the means to a better end, within them." Mike quickly scanned the room, looking to all of the children of the Domains and saw those same small smiles he had seen so many times when they were talking among themselves. He felt Gloreana's hand close on his arm and he glanced to her. He saw that she too was surveying the room and that she too, had seen the smiles. Mike looked to the Corsendorian Prince's and saw those same smiles on their faces.

"They're talking to our children," Gloreana whispered and looked to him. He smiled with his nod.

"All during the battle with the Dark Forces, these children argued that we must join in the defeat of the Dark One, but our ways of peace are deeply ingrained, and we stayed hidden," King Cranedoran stated. "When the Dark

One was defeated, these children pressed that we make ourselves known to the Overseer and the other Domains, but we worried of what you would think of our ways and we hesitated." The looks now shared throughout the room, ran from regret to anger. "It was my two sons, Prince Crendosa and Prince Crondasa, that presented to me the only argument that gave a true reason that we should make ourselves known," Cranedoran stated. "The peoples of Corsendora and our life style, had become stalled. We no longer sought new goals. We no longer thirsted for life, but steadily maintained a civilization of routine and unknowingly, boredom. We needed to join with the rightful Domains and bring life back to Corsendora and that might mean that we may have to fight, but we would be fighting for life." Everyone looked to the two prince's, who now stood in front of their parents and everyone saw that they had not heard one word of what their father had said. The boys, when not talking to the other young, were too lost in Maelie's and Brie's eyes and were talking with them!

CHAPTER ONE

Many years had passed since the war with Palakrine. In those years, there had been many who had lost their battle with time, and there had been many that had taken up the fight with their birth. Mike, the Overseer of the Realm, could remember the passing of each. Especially his son, Zachia, who had gone after Saltakrine alone, and had paid the ultimate price for that foolishness. Zachia had killed Saltakrine, and his son Balakrine, but there had been another, and that one had killed Zachia. Tommy, the most powerful of the sensitive's, had said that he had sensed this killer as a girl.

Mike was working at his desk and trying to ignore the ache in his back, when Palysee and Drandysee arrived at the palace. Mike was pleased to see his old friend and his student. "Palysee, Drandysee, it is good to see you both," Mike said forcing himself to his feet and giving the traditional greeting, which included hand clasping and a bow. His back did not appreciate the effort. Palysee and Drandysee returned the greeting. Mike noticed that there seemed a confliction of emotions in the eyes of the Wingless. "Please sit my friends." Mike indicated the chairs that faced the desk. "What brings you two on this beautiful day Palysee?" Mike asked after they had settled in the chairs. Palysee didn't meet his eyes at first, but eventually lifted them to Mike's.

"We have found another Domain; we have found another Domain," Palysee sang simply and Mike lifted his right brow. "It is a small one, but like the Plain, it is a powerful one; it is a small one, but like the Plain, it is a powerful one." Mike looked to him, knowing what was coming. Mike was near seventy now and although his health was good, he knew that many were wondering how long he would be able to keep the position of Overseer.

"And what have you found in this Domain Palysee?" Mike asked calmly. Palysee dropped his eyes for a moment. "Come my old friend. We have been together to long to hide from each other." Mike smiled as Palysee met his eyes again. The Elder smiled and nodded.

"A young human at fourteen years, with powers very close to your own at that age; a young human at fourteen years, with powers very close to your own at that age," Palysee song told him and Mike nodded. He glanced at the unemotional face of Drandysee and then back to Palysee.

"Do you feel that this youth has the potential of becoming the new Overseer?" Mike asked quietly. Palysee slowly nodded, never taking his eyes from Mike's. "Fourteen years old, you say?" Again Palysee nodded. Their conversation was abruptly interrupted by the echoing scream of Natoria, the elf who had conceded her elfin long life, to wed his younger brother, Morgan. Mike surprised himself at the speed at which he cleared his chair and ran up the stairs to Morgan and Natoria's rooms. He burst into the room and ran to the balcony, where he stopped still. He looked to the sobbing Natoria, on her knees between the feet of the two loungers and holding the joined hands of Megan and Morgan. Gloreana gasped as she took Mike's arm, having just arrived. Morgan and Megan lay on loungers, side by side. Their ankles were crossed comfortably. Their gray haired heads were resting on the slightly reclined back of the loungers, their eyes closed and a small smile on each of their faces. They looked simply asleep, but the sobbing of Natoria told all that the twins, who were identical, except for gender, had passed on together, holding hands. Gloreana went to the elf and held her as the racking sobs shook her. Mike could not stop the tears of his heart break and they fell freely from his eyes as he looked to his younger brother and sister.

As the residents of the palace gathered, the word was quickly spread to all Domains. The scattered children rushed to the palace and wept with their shared loss. It would be some time before Mike and Palysee had the opportunity to discuss this young man Palysee had found, because not six months after Morgan and Megan's passing, Katie, Mike's biological twin, so bereaved from Jarpon's death, a year earlier, and the sudden loss of both her younger brother and sister, passed away from her mourning. Marie, a close cousin to Mike and Katie and the twins who had passed, followed her within three months and her husband Quentloe, followed her within days. Mike was now the only one left of the five who had freed the Realm and Domains of the terrors of Maltakrine's and Palakrine's Dark Magic.

Mike was having trouble concentrating and his heart ached with the loss of his brother and sisters, as well as his cousin. Gloreana tried to give him support, but she too felt the loss of those who had become family to her. They were not alone, for the entire family, wide spread, fought with the losses of their loved ones. Because of the ramifications of the losses of loved ones and the adjustments that were needed for the heirs of the different Domains, it was years before Mike and Palysee could again sit down and discuss the boy that had been found, but even then, a shadow hung over all.

Mike tried to listen to Palysee as he was given the report of the boy, but his mind was on Gloreana's weakening condition. "His powers have grown with him, as did yours; his powers have grown with him, as did yours." Palysee sang to Mike. "Perhaps you could bring the boy here, for a talk; perhaps you could bring the boy here, for a talk?" Palysee's song asked the Overseer. "Then you could decide for yourself; then you could decide for yourself." Mike nodded, but his mind could not be pulled from Gloreana, who now rested in their bedroom, under the care of Pelidora. "Mike; Mike?" Palysee asked, watching his eyes. Mike looked to him and then sat up straighter in his chair.

"I'm sorry Palysee," Mike told him and the Elder shook his head.

"There is no need for apology Mike; there is no need of apology Mike," he sang gently. "I know that you worry for Gloreana; I know that you worry for Gloreana. We all do; we all do." Palysee's song was soft. Mike smiled at his old friend.

"I will send a message to this Domain, telling of our ambassadors arrival. Then I will send Zandian and Renoria to meet the people of this Domain and talk with their leader. Then I will call the boy here," he said and Palysee nodded.

"That is a wise decision my friend; that is a wise decision my friend," The elder sang and stood. "Please let me know what happens; please let me know what happens." Palysee sang quietly, as he and Drandysee bowed, and they left. Mike stared at his desk for a moment and then called Heather and the children of Zachia and Sen, to him. When Heather had arrived and had been told of Mike's desires, she began searching and she quickly found that she could talk with several of the Domain and learned some of the names the brother and sister would need. She told her father that the ones she had talked with seemed to be seers and talkers, and they had been waiting for her to contact them. Mike nodded and looked to his grandchildren, Renoria and Zandian.

"I'm going to send you two to establish a joining with this Domain." They nodded. "I want you to observe what the

Domain is like and what we can expect from their leader. I also want to know about this boy."

"Don't worry grandpa," Renoria said with a small grin. "We know what you want and we will not fail you," she told him gently. Mike nodded and looked to Heather.

"let them know they're coming," he told her and she nodded as she called to those of the Domain and then told her niece and nephew, the names of the ones they needed to talk with. When Heather received the word that the leader had been told of their arrival and where they should appear, Mike spelled them to the Domain. It was four hours later that he spelled them back and they had much to tell him. A month of talks with Palysee and Drandysee, as well as Elamson, the ruler of Calisonnos and Mike finally sent word that he wanted Namson to come to the Realm.

<hr />

Castope, granddaughter of Saltakrine, daughter of Balakrine, looked out from her balcony at the wonder that was the city started by her grandfather. She could hear the harsh breathing of her son, Dremlon, behind her. He knew to stand behind her and not even with her for she ruled, not him. She knew the story of her history by heart, for her father and grandfather had drummed it into her. She would be the one to do what the others' of Dark Magic could not. The history she had been told, was the foretelling of her future. The future of the Dark Magic, that she now controlled. As her father had told her, Saltakrine had said that it would be a daughter of the Dark Magic that would rule the Realm and she was the first female born to that power since Saltakrine's sister. She knew how Saltakrine had fought to live, after the greedy one had tried to destroy him. How he had brought the creature Starle with him as well as any of the forces he could find, left from his father's failed attempt to take the Realm. He had found many more than he had expected. How he had grown up on that barren planet until he was strong enough to find a better Domain. He had finally found one that suited his expectations and brought all to this Domain and began the building of the Dark City. Finding lesser sorcerers and sorceresses of the Dark Magic, of different Domains and recruiting them.

How he had tried to mate Starle with a sorceress and found that Starle was incapable of impregnating a female of any kind. Repeated attempts were made and nothing. Starle's death had come as a complete surprise to him. So Saltakrine commanded that as she was the first female of the Dark power, she was to mate a Demon first. She was to try to mate the son she bore with a sorceress and see if that made the difference. It had, for Dremlon had so far, created several offspring from sorceresses and one from a captured female elf. The only differences between Dremlon and his offspring was that the offspring didn't have the demons horns and the fact that their power in the Dark Magic was stronger. She called these offspring Dremlors. A race of sorcerers and sorceresses that had more power and were completely obedient to her. Castope was mating the boy as fast as she could.

She had just come from the third attempt to get pregnant from the Elfin male, the mate of the female impregnated by her son. She had enjoyed the sex with the elf, unlike the Demon. The Demon hadn't lasted long enough to even interest her, though it had only taken one time and she had gotten pregnant.

Castope continued her scanning of the city as her thoughts wandered. She had been told what the Realm should look like and she longed for the chance to see it directly. She had been warned by her father and Saltakrine, to wait until she was very sure of her power, before she did anything about taking the Realm. She looked to the cliffs, just a few miles from her castle. The caves she could see there, held the population of Fire Dragons, now over sixty in number, that her grandfather, her father, and now she, so carefully nursed back from extinction. She smiled as she thought of the power of the creatures killing instinct. "I will not fail you grandfather," she said softly as she thought of the night her grandfather and father had been killed by the son of the Overseer, the one called Zachia. She remembered the pleasure she had felt, killing that one, but she had worried about the sudden disappearance of the body. She was determined that the Overseer and his entire family owed her more than they could ever pay. A sorceress, Ragella, came to the balcony. She was known to be a seer.

"What is it Ragella?" Castope asked patiently, without turning very far.

"Mistress," she said softly. Castope turned the rest of the way to her. "There is an elf and he is looking for Saltakrine." Dremlon looked to Castope, she tried to ignore him.

"Why would an elf be looking for us?" he asked her with a smirk.

"He possesses Dark Magic," the seer told them both, as Castope gave a harsh look at her son.

"No elf possesses Dark Magic," Castope told the seer, with a sneer.

"This one does and he seeks the ruler of the Dark Forces," the sorceress told her. Castope saw the seer turn from her glare.

"Give me your seeing," Castope told her and Ragella closed her eyes and passed her seeing to her. Castope made a gesture and muttered a spell and Morsalon, son of Mensalon and Charlesia, stood before her. She quickly scanned his form and she liked what she saw. She could clearly see that he copied her actions. She didn't know that he was only half elf and he never bothered to tell her and that fact led to later situations.

───────⚜───────

Namson looked to his father with very wide eyes. It was his sixteenth birthday and his father had just told him something that was the best of presents possible. He tried to ignore the worried look that had come to his mother's eyes. "Could you say that again my father?" he asked, afraid that it would not be said the same. Elamson grinned into his son's bright eyes.

"The Overseer has requested that you come to the Realm, for a personal conference," Elamson stated. Namson felt pride in himself when he saw his father's chest swell even more with the pride he felt for him.

"Did this Overseer say why he wanted Namson or what this conference was about?" Ferlinos asked none to quietly, causing Namson to smile secretly. Elamson glared at his wife.

"It would matter not woman," he told her and she returned his glare. Namson continued to hide the grin that had come to him.

"It does to me," she told him calmly, but forcefully. The others' gathered for the birthday party, smiled with the exchange. All knew the power of Elamson's control of their Domain, but they also knew of the power of his wife.

"Mama, don't worry," Namson said soothingly. "It has only been a month now since the Realms first contact. It is a honor for the Overseer to call for me. I go with the eagerness and the pride of all Calisonnos!" Namson returned his sight to his father, but out of the corner of his eyes, he saw his mother look to him and he could see that she fought between her misunderstood fear of what was to be and her love and pride of him. Gerpinos just glared at her older brother, something that Namson was not ignoring. "Papa?" Namson asked quietly. "Why don't you ask the Overseer if we all could visit the Realm?" Ferlinos and Gerpinos brightened immediately. His father had a moment of surprise and then looked disappointedly at his son. Namson almost smiled at his father's reply.

"And who would tend to Calisonnos?" Elamson asked sternly and his wife and daughter frowned at him. Namson looked from his father's eyes for a moment, gathering his thoughts and then return to them.

"Minister Monason can tend Calisonnos for a few days my father." Monason looked at him in surprise. "All know what your wrath would bring if they disobeyed the laws," Namson said with a slight grin. He could easily see the nodding heads and lifted brows around the room. Elamson looked around in a glance and all sobered immediately. Elamson looked to his son.

"I will consider this idea," he said officially. Namson glanced at his sister and winked. She smiled with her head down, so her father could not see.

"You know that none would disobey, my father," Namson pushed. Elamson glared at his son. Namson did not drop his eyes this time. "Papa, you know you are curious to see the Realm, would you deny this?" Elamson's glare increased, but Namson pushed on. "The truth papa. The same thing you ask of all Calisonnos." Anger flashed in Elamson's eyes for a split second and then he calmed.

"I think it a proper and wise idea my husband," Ferlinos stated and Elamson looked to her, so he did not see the grin Namson gave his sister. "You would have the chance to speak directly with the Overseer, about our needs and wants," she added, returning his look evenly. Elamson stared at her for a few minutes and she never wavered. He slowly turned his eyes to his Minister.

"Monason," the Minister looked to him. "You will make sure that the laws are obeyed by all!" Monason nodded, so did Namson, as he glanced at his grinning mother and sister.

"Yes my lord," Monason stated, trying not to smile, as most of the room struggled with the same problem. Elamson nodded and turned to Dulanos.

"Tell the Realm that all of my family will be coming when we are told of the time." The one who could best talk to those of the Realm nodded and concentrated.

"Papa, why not use the orb that was given to us?" Namson asked, somehow managing not to grin as he did so. Elamson glared at him. His mother and sister did not succeed as well and had to turn from their husband and father, to hide their grins.

CHAPTER TWO

Castope continued to finalize the building of her Dark City, and her plans for the Realm. Morsalon, the half elfin son of Charlesia and Mensalon, was able to help in more than just the maps of Realm City and the surrounding areas, he could also help her with children. Castope's hand rested on her swollen abdomen as she looked from the balcony. She looked down to her belly and smiled. This was the second child she would bear from Morsalon. Dremlon had tried to sway her from keeping the elf, but she had just simply ignored him and kept him busy breeding sorceresses. There were now at least seventy five of the young Dremlors, with a greater Dark Magic power than her best sorcerers and at least twenty pregnant sorceresses, several for the third time. She smiled with the knowledge that her grandfather had been so right. She was unaware that there were some that plotted as she did, but not for the same outcome.

"Castope," Cartope called as she came to the balcony. Castope turned to her daughter, the first of the children Morsalon had planted within her and now near ten years old. She did not let the girl call her mama. She couldn't stand the word.

"What is it?" she asked the girl. She saw that the girl was mad about something and she had a good idea what angered her.

"Morsalon!" Cartope exclaimed. Castope almost smiled.

"What now?" she asked calmly, still in the good mood about how well her plans were coming together. Cartope stopped short of her and glared.

"He still tries to tell me what I should do!" Castope actually sighed.

"What did he tell you to do?" she asked, still calm. Cartope hesitated.

"Not what I am to do now, but that I must start to prepare to be mated to one of those stinking Demons." The girl stomped her foot. "I do not want one of those things touching me," she added. Castope lost her good mood. She looked to the girl and her eyes turned hard.

"When you are old enough, you will be mated with a Demon and there is no doubt of this," she told her. Cartope looked surprised and then angry.

"Why?" she demanded and Castope came to her, taking both her arms in her hands and she was not gentle about it, causing Cartope to wince.

"Because you will birth one like Dremlon and that one will breed with those Dremlon has created, and that will give us ones with even greater Dark Magical power!," Castope told her.

"But I hate those beasts," the girl cried out. Castope tightened her grip and Cartope winced again.

"You will do as I command," she told her daughter harshly; "and that is the end of it!" She shoved the girl. "Now attend your instructress and leave me in peace." Castope turned back to the sight of her city that was getting bigger and better daily. She heard the mutterings of Cartope as the girl went to her classes. Her good humor returned. "Yes grandfather, I will make the Realm, and all who are of it, pay for what they have done," she told the city. It didn't answer her, and she didn't care.

Mike, Heather and Tyrus, Trayton and Chrystal, appeared in the main hall, returning from Semitor's funeral. The close friend of Mike and the retired General of the Armies, of Ventoria, had passed away in the night, following the burial of his mate Pelsikor. Jardan and Dana, of the North West Domain, who had attended the funeral representing all of Vistalin, had returned to the North West Domain. Mike immediately started for the stairs. Heather placed her hand on his arm, stopping him. He looked to her, questioning.

"Are you alright daddy?" she asked quietly. He put his hand on hers and tried to smile.

"I want to check on your mother and I will be fine," he told her. She nodded and removed her hand slowly. Tyrus came and put his arm around her shoulders. She glanced at him and then turned back and watched her father go up the stairs.

"Let's get a brandy." Tyrus said quietly and pulled ever so gently on her shoulders.

"I agree," Trayton said and headed for the reading room. Heather took one last look to the balcony and followed Tyrus's guiding.

Mike entered the bedroom and immediately saw the sadness of those who tended Gloreana. He went to the bed, sitting gently as he took Gloreana's hand. He sighed with relief when she opened her eyes and smiled softly at him.

"My lord, my time has come," she whispered. Mike started to slowly shake his head as tears began to come to his eyes. "No My Lord, do not weep for me. We have done more than even we thought we could. We have made very special children who follow our lead and teach their children what they have learned from us." Gloreana took a shaky breath and lifted her other hand and touched his cheek. "We have shared more than any other could dream of. I will always be yours." Her eyes closed and her hand that had been touching his cheek, fell to the bed. He continued to hold her other hand, staring into her closed eyes as tears poured from his. The sounds of the others' weeping were the only sound in the room. In the reading room, Heather gasped and dropped her glass.

Tyrus looked to her and did not need to be told. He took her into his arms and held her as she sobbed. The others bowed their heads and wept with her. In all the Domains, the loss was felt and the tears of sorrow overwhelmed them all. Mike placed Gloreana's tomb in the center of the flower garden she had loved so much. It was a week after the funeral that Mike called to Calisonnos and told them to prepare, for the next day they were to come to the Realm.

Heather, Tyrus, Talyus, Renoria, Crandora and Trayton stood to Mike's right. King Cranedoran, Queen Xanaloren, Quansloe and Hannah, Jardan and Dana on his left. They all stood on the front terrace, waiting for the portal to open. Inside the entrance hall, there were many gathered, as well as in the reception room. On the balcony at the top of the stairs, overlooking the rest, stood Glornina and her parents, Sonilon and Ventia and her grandmother, Chrystal. As hard as Ventia and Chrystal tried, they could not stop Glornina from resting her forearms on the railing, in less than a lady like, bent position. Sonilon finally told them to leave her be and they all settled, though both Ventia and Chrystal would occasionally glare at the fifteen, very close to sixteen year old girl.

Glornina was something of a particular amazement to all who had known Gloreana, for she bore a striking resemblance to her great grandmother. Her hair was a shining black and wavy, just as Gloreana's had been. She was a powerful seer, as her great grandmother had been.

Her complexion, though not as dark as Gloreana's, was still darker than any of her relatives and her beauty easily equaled her great grandmothers. As she rested her arms on the railing and looked out over all those gathered below her, a small, secretive smile, rested comfortably on the corners of her mouth. Whispered words, traveling through the crowd below, told them that the visitors had arrived.

"For pity sake Glornina, please stand up," Ventia tried one more time. The girl ignored her, but her smile had become more pronounced.

There had been considerable discussion, on Calisonnos, on the order of persons through the portal. Elamson said, as ruler, he should lead. Ferlinos informed him that since Namson was the one who had been invited and Elamson was just tagging along, the boy should be first. The look in Ferlinos's eyes made it clear that she was right and Elamson was smart enough not to argue too much. Though at first, he had tried, a little. In the end, Namson led the visitors from the portal. Fifteen year old Gerpinos was mad that she was forced to bring up the rear of the parade, as her parents followed her older brother. As it turned out, she found she liked her position best. For, it was after several people had been introduced to her, that she saw the most intensely blue eyes she had ever seen. She was hooked to those eyes from that point on!

Mike watched as Palysee and Drandysee greeted the visitors as the portal closed behind them. They led them, one to each side of Namson, through the gate and to the terrace where Mike awaited them. The Overseer smiled as he watched Elamson reaction of surprise at the meeting with the Wingless, and the actions of the woman with him as she quickly settled the Ruler. Mike almost joined the giggling of the girl following, at her father's behavior. Mike smiled and gave a short nod as he looked at the boy. Namson walked with a simple strength that did not need words to enforce. Mike estimated that the boy was at least six foot tall and was obviously well muscled. His hair was brown, as were the rest of those in the party. His eyes matched his hair, but as the boy neared, Mike saw a mischievous sparkle in them.

―――⁓⋄⋆⊙⋆⋄⁓―――

"May I present The Overseer of the Realm; may I present The Overseer of The Realm," Palysee sang, after they had stopped, just short of the steps to the terrace, indicating Mike and backing slightly. Namson bowed, with Elamson, Ferlinos and Gerpinos following his lead. Mike returned the bow, even though his back complained about it.

"It is an honor to meet you Lord Overseer," Namson said as he bowed. Mike was impressed that the boys voice was steady, with no hint of hesitation, and he had never dropped his eyes from Mike's.

"It is my honor to meet you and your family," Mike said as they again stood erect. Heather and Talyus both heard the very slight strain in his voice, from the bow.

"Daddy?" Heather asked in his mind.

"I'm fine," he told her in like manner and began the introductions. "May I present my daughter Heather and her husband Tyrus, the Keeper of Magic of the North East Domain of Vistalin." Both Heather and Tyrus bowed and Namson and his family responded. Mike was pleased to see that Namson did not take his eyes from those he greeted. Mike turned to the first two to his left. "Their majesties, King Cranedoran and his queen, Xanaloren, of the Domain Corsendora" The bows by both sides. As they stood up Elamson whispered to Ferlinos.

"That should be my title, when we return to Calisonnos." Ferlinos elbowed his side, hard, as Mike fought his smile at the Calisonnos leaders actions. Then his eyes caught the eyes of the daughter behind Elamson, as he shot a quick glare at Ferlinos. Mike again fought his grin as the girl grinned at her father and let her eyes wander. Mike saw the girls eyes open wide and Mike quickly looked over his shoulder and saw the son of Renoria and Crandora, looking intently back at the girl. Without looking to her directly, Mike could see that the girl was reacting to the movements of her parents as she bowed, but she was definitely lost in Vandora's eyes. Mike swung his arm back to the right.

"My youngest son Talyus." Mike continued and bows were exchanged. Back to the left, "Quansloe, The Keeper of The Plain, and his wife Hannah." Bows were made. Heather and Talyus again heard a tone to their fathers voice, but this one they understood. They knew he had thoughts of his father. To the right again, "Renoria, the oldest daughter of Senfarna, the widow of my late son Zachia, and her husband Crandora, of Corsendora." Again a catch was heard in Mike's voice that all understood. Bows were given. Back to the left. "Jardan, The Keeper of Magic for the North West Domain and The Keeper of all Magic for Vistalin, and his wife Jardana." Bows were again exchanged. To the right. "My nephew, Trayton." Bows were made.

"It is an honor to meet you all," Namson said, before Elamson could even open his mouth. Ferlinos grinned slightly, as did Mike as he caught a glimpse of the look on Elamson's face. He could also see that the girl didn't care. She seemed to stay with the young man's eyes and that was all she wanted, for now. "May I present my father, Elamson, Ruler of Calisonnos and my mother Ferlinos." Bows were made by all, including Mike and his back liked this one even less than the first. "My younger sister, Gerpinos." Namson stated, as he indicated the girl with his hand. Ferlinos had to nudge the girl, who did not want to give up possession of those eyes. She tore herself from them and quickly bowed and returned to the blue ocean she desired. Mike's bow was not quite as deep as before. His back had said that's enough and refused to bend very much.

"Come," Mike stated; "we have arranged a reception with those of all the Domains. Please follow me." Mike pointed to the door and Namson nodded and stepped forward.

Mike indicated that the boy should walk with him and the rest followed them through the large door, into the palace proper. Mike heard the Ruler of Calisonnos next words and had to fight his laughter as to the reaction of his wife.

"I should have a palace like this," Elamson whispered and got elbowed again for his thoughts. As they came through the door, Glornina slowly began to straighten, much to the delight of her mother and grandmother, though they did not know the reason for the girls actions. Glornina's eyes met those of Namson.

"At last, he's here," she stated softly and ran down the stairs. Ventia and Chrystal had heard what she had said. They looked to each other and whispered the same words, in unison; "Of shit!" Sonilon chuckled as he watched his daughter. Both women turned to him and glared. Glornina pushed her way through the crowd of people and then suddenly stood in front of Namson, who had been watching her progress with considerable interest. She broke through and stopped in front of him. They both smiled, as on the balcony, Ventia and Chrystal gasped and looked to Sonilon, who was smiling.

"My name is Glornina and I welcome you to the Realm," she said rather loudly. Mike's eyes opened wide at the sudden appearance of his great granddaughter. Namson smiled and reached for her hand. As he drew it to him, he bowed and placed a gentle kiss and then stood.

"I am Namson and I am very, very, pleased to meet you," he told her quite softly. Glornina blushed slightly as a knowing smile came to more than just Mike's face. Elamson frowned at his son's behavior, while Ferlinos beamed with the pride of her son. No one looked to see Gerpinos's reaction. Mike indicated that they should proceed into the reception room. Glornina took Namson's side, not letting go of his hand, that did not seem to want to let go of hers, and they entered the room.

———

When they stopped in the center of the room, Mike called for quiet and silence quickly descended.

"Rather than go through the tedious efforts of introducing each other, one by one, I suggest that we just intermingle and allow each to introduce themselves to our guests. Glornina, perhaps you could accompany Namson and introduce him to those gathered?" Mike suggested with a wink at her. She blushed again as she nodded and pulled the willing young man off. "Elamson, perhaps you would allow me to introduce you and your wife to those who have come here today?" Elamson nodded his head. Ferlinos looked around and suddenly realized that her daughter was not where she was supposed to be, with her! She reached out and tugged on Elamson's sleeve. He looked to her with irritation for the interruption.

"Where is Gerpinos?" she asked in a hoarse whisper. Elamson looked around and shrugged. She glared at him. Mike had over heard her question and he too looked around. He finally turned to her, remembering the looks exchanged between Gerpinos and Vandora.

"There is no one here that would harm her. I'm sure she is just looking around and will rejoin you soon. Don't worry," he told the concerned mother. Ferlinos looked to him and then around the room again, letting herself be pulled along by Elamson.

On the other side of the room, near the door, Namson stood, holding Glornina's hand. He turned to her and was about to say something, when her fingers touched his lips, stopping him from speaking. She came closer to him and slid her arms around his neck. She reached up with her lips and he bent slightly and their lips touched. It took some time for the kiss to end and when it did, they were both flushed and short of breath. She neither blushed nor turned her eyes from his as she spoke; "I know a place of privacy," she told him and he smiled.

"Lead me where you would," he told her. She grinned and pulled him out the door.

In the reading room, for Vandora had gently pulled the willing girl from the group and had brought her around the rear of the crowd and into this room, Gerpinos turned to the eyes that had led her here and smiled. The boy backed the door closed still holding her hand and she didn't see him reach behind him and lock the door. She wouldn't have cared if she had. "My name is Vandora," he told her as he drew closer to her. Her heart began to beat faster at his nearness.

"I am Gerpinos," she tried to say with a regular voice, looking into the boys intense blue eyes. He smiled when it came out as a whisper. He took her other hand and he stopped just short of touching his body with hers. She smiled into his eyes and pulled the hands that held hers, drawing him to her. Their lips neared and then they were kissing. Gently at first, but it soon intensified. Gerpinos's arms encircled his neck and his went around her waist. She could not believe the physical excitement she felt. She suddenly felt his excitement press against her. His arm went behind her legs and he picked her up into his arms. They did not break the kiss as he carried her to the large couch.

⸺⁓◦◦⁊◉◦◉⁊◦◦⁓⸺

Two hours later, Ferlinos finally saw her daughter, her hand inside the arm of a boy. She tensed with the beginning of anger. When the two stopped in front of her, she saw the flush on Gerpinos's cheeks and a sparkle in her eyes. Her anger built. "Mother, this is Vandora, son of Renoria and Crandora. Vandora, my mother Ferlinos." Ferlinos turned her angry eyes to the boy and almost physically jumped at the intensity of the blue eyes that looked back. Vandora reach for Ferlinos's hand, bent at the waist and gently kissed her hand. Ferlinos looked to her smiling daughter and all anger left her. She returned her daughters smile.

"It is an honor to meet the lovely mother of this beautiful woman," Vandora said softly, as he straightened, with a very knowing smile on his lips. Ferlinos couldn't think of a thing to say and Gerpinos giggled. Just minutes later, Ferlinos saw her son, with Glornina's arm through his and she wore the same glow her daughter had worn. She couldn't stop her happy smile of pride. Elamson, not having the slightest idea of what had happened with his children, thought she had lost her mind, and she didn't care.

⁓⁓⁓⁓⁕⁕⁕⁕⁕⁕⁕⁕⁕⁕⁕⁕⁕⁕⁕⁕⁕⁕⁕⁕⁓⁓⁓⁓

There was knock on Castope's office door. She and Morsalon had been going over the layout of Realm City and the surrounding area, again. She wanted, and needed, to know everything about the Realm she could learn. Castope sighed angrily. "What is it now?" she called out. Ragella opened the door carefully. "Come in!" Castope yelled. Ragella stepped into the room, her head bowed. "Well?" Castope asked.

"Mistress, the new Overseer trainee has arrived in the Realm." Castope smiled for the first time that day. She waved the sorceress away and grinned at the map they had been making.

"A new Overseer," Morsalon exclaimed; "that will ruin our plans." Castope looked to him in exasperation.

"Did you think that the Overseer would just die and there would be none to replace him?" she asked sarcastically. Morsalon looked to her, his eyes blank.

"Males," Castope sighed and rose from her chair. "Go see to the training of the troops. Perhaps you can be a value to me that way," she snapped and left the room. Morsalon fumed for several minutes and then had an idea. He left the room and headed for the class room of Castope's two daughters. He was getting very tired of her treatment of him. He needed an ally. The youngest girl, Prateope, just recently born, was too young to really learn anything directly, but Castope had insisted that she be placed in the room. She said the girl would learn, without having to be taught. Morsalon had not understood, but it was Cartope he wanted to talk with, for she was no happier with her mother than Morsalon was.

———※※◈※◈◈※◈◇◆※※———

In a quiet, secretive part of Dark City, Somora, one of the first Dremlors born, talked with his followers. They listened to his thoughts of their escape from the rule of Castope. They smiled and nodded as he told them of their future.

———※※◈※◈◈※◈◇◆※※———

Grembo, Grames and Grittle were sitting at the table in their cabin, with Gratable and Gromlee, the parents of Grimnoa, wife of Manable. They were all excited because Gremble and his entire family were coming for a visit. It had been many years since the last visit and although they had been kept informed of pairings and births, this was the first time that they would get to meet the entire family, all at once and in person. Grembo was showing a considerable amount of gray hair now and both Grames and Grittle would tease him about it, but only so far. He still had a powerful temper. Gromlee had to use both hands to drink from her mug for her hands shook with her excitement of seeing her daughter again.

"Gromlee," Gratable said teasingly; "can't you control yourself at all?" She glared at him and then smiled to Grames and Grittle.

"It has been so long since I have seen her, maybe I can't," she told them and they chuckled as Grames held up her hand and they all saw that it trembled as well.

"Females," Grembo muttered to Gratable and he chuckled.

"Hold up your hand oh great Grembo!" Grames said with irritation in her voice. He glared at her and then it turned to a grin, shaking his head slowly. They all laughed at the leader of the ogres of Plain.

"When are they to come?" Gromlee asked Grames, for Grames had been the one who had received the message from Gremble, by way of a faxlie, from Quansloe.

"He said not long after sunrise." Grames answered with a smile. "I wonder what keeps Grastable and Graminel? Grandoa will be disappointed if they are not here."

"They have much farther to travel," Gromlee said; "but, you can be sure that Graminel would not miss a visit with her daughter." Grames and Grittle chuckled as they nodded their agreement.

"Then let us finish our drinks out at the table in the yard," Grembo said rising from his chair. The rest nodded and they all took their mugs and went outside to the table both Grames and Grittle had insisted they get, after their visit to the Valley. They settled at the table and Gromlee looked around and grinned.

"Maybe we should have a table outside too Gratable," she said. Gratable frowned and gave Grembo a *now see what you've done,* look. Grames and Grittle laughed at him. Hermusa and Peslamir strolled into the clearing. Hermusa, the biggest of the great grandsons of Hermus and Cellus, was now the lead ram of the sheep herd. They stopped near the table and bowed to Grembo and the others. The ogres returned the bows with a nod of their heads.

"We have come to meet the son of Grembo and his family," Hermusa said after lifting from his bow.

"You are welcome Hermusa and Peslamir," Grembo stated. "They should be here anytime now, we hope!" Not had those words but cleared Grembo's mouth that a portal opened and Gremble led his family to the home of his youth. Grames jumped up and hurried to her son. She threw her arms around him, burying her head onto his shoulder. Grittle was right behind her and she too hugged her welcome to her half son. Grimnoa did the same with her mother and then her father. Grembo came to his son and extended his hand. Gremble looked to him and clasp his forearm and Grembo grabbed his sons forearm. They exchanged smiles and nods.

"Have they come yet?" an excited voice called out as Grastable and Graminel rushed into the clearing. Grastable was puffing loudly. Grandoa cried out in joy and met her parents before they had reached the group. After several minutes of joyful welcomes, Gremble lined his family up and began the introductions to the seven parents, grandparents and now, great grandparents. There were four they already knew, but the rest they did not. Gremble walked behind the line, Grandoa with him, a smile of pride on her face and in her eyes.

"You all remember our son, Manable." Gremble started, stopping behind his son. "Well, he is slightly larger than he was at the last meeting." Manable blushed slightly as the ones facing them grinned and nodded, their eyes wide. Grembo's chest swelled with the pride of his grandson who was now slightly bigger than his father. Gremble moved on. "You all remember Grimnoa and you can see that she glows with motherhood." Grimnoa blushed, a lot, while Gratable and Gromlee beamed at their daughter. Gremble moved to the next. "Allow me to introduce you to Morgable, Manable and Grimnoa's son and your great grandson." Grames, Grittle and Graminel exchanged wide eyed looks. Gremble looked to Gratable and Gromlee. "And your grandson." He moved to the next in line. "This lovely thing is Minstoa, our daughter." He announced and Minstoa bowed. Gremble moved on. "This young ogre is her mate, Grable!" Grable bowed as he took his mates hand. "This sweet little thing is Meathoa, their daughter." Meathoa grabbed her father's leg and buried her face in the hair of his side, for she was taller than his waist. Everyone laughed at the child's shyness. Gremble nudged his daughter and she grinned. "I have to mention that

Minstoa is again with young!" The seven moved forward, Grames and Grittle going first to Minstoa. All of the females gave hugs to the new family members as the males gave the arm clasp to the new males and hugs to the females. It took some time for Meathoa to loosen enough for the hugs that the seven so wanted to give, but within a couple of hours, she was as comfortable with them as she was with her parents. Though, just after lunch, she had a small fit when the Great Eagles landed. Marlar and his mate Ralitan, were even bigger than Vralar and Nilitan, the King and Queen of the eagles of the Realm. Marlar had come to the Plain when the news of Kraslar's death reached the Realm, to assume the role of King of the Plains Great Eagles, as Kraslar's great grandson.

"We came to welcome your family to the Plain and to visit with our friends." Marlar stated and both Gremble and Grandoa smiled as they bowed their heads. Ralitan looked to Meathoa and bowed to the child.

"You need not fear us young one, we are friends of your great grandfathers and great grandmothers," she told the child, who peeked at them from behind her father. Grable nudged the child out into the open.

"Come daughter, say hello to our friends," he urged her gently. Meathoa looked at the eagles for a moment.

"Hello," she said barely loud enough to be heard. Both eagles bowed to her and she began to smile. The Eagles could not stay long, as they were beginning a hunt. A young ewe arrived and went to Hermusa and whispered to him. He nodded and came to Grembo and Gremble as Peslamir went to those a who had settled around the table. He wore a tired expression.

"I fear we must leave. There seems to be a question concerning two rams and one ewe and she can't seem to make up her mind. Needless to say, the rams have decided to settle the matter themselves and I think the ewe is the problem," he told them with a half grin. Both ogres smiled and nodded. They bid farewell to the sheep, feeling sympathy for Hermusa.

"How goes the Realm?" Grembo asked his son, as they moved to two sitting stones, not far from the rest that sat at the outside table. Gremble didn't answer right away and Grembo looked to him, questioningly. Gremble sighed deeply.

"There has been many lost in the years." Grembo nodded his knowledge of those losses. "Morgan's death was hard for me to deal with." Grembo nodded, knowing the bond his son had had with the younger brother of Mike. "The death of Zachia shook all Domains. It was so senseless that he would have taken on Saltakrine alone." Again Grembo nodded, looking to the ground. "The loss of Gloreana was devastating to all, especially Mike." Grembo looked to his son and waited. "I think he realizes his time is coming, for he has taken a boy into the palace and trains him to take his place as Overseer." Grembo nodded his understanding of the need of this. Ogres lived much longer than humans. "There was a half elf, the son of Charlesia and Mensalon, who had turned to Dark Magic, tried to kill his father Mensalon, and has disappeared." Grembo lifted his brows, for he had not heard of this event. "Elamson, the ruler of the Domain Calisonnos and the father of the boy Mike trains, has invited any ogres who wish, to come to his Domain. I think he does this to try and use ogres to control his people much more. I had heard that his mate, Ferlinos, was angry about the invitation, for the same reason." Grembo straightened and looked to Gremble.

"I hope you are stopping this," Grembo said. Gremble shook his head and looked to his father, a small grin on one corner of his mouth.

"After I learned of the wife's anger, I talked with Ferlinos and I asked for volunteers and Manable and his family plus Grisble and his family, as well as a few more did so." Grembo tried to think why the name Grisble sounded familiar and Gremble smiled more. "Grisble was the child who beat the young but full grown Crouse near to death when Crouse tried to burn down his parents cabin, and took Graddle's place to lure Balteen and the Demons. He was the one to represent Graddle, when the Overseer sent the Demons back to Demonsar," Gremble reminded his father. Grembo smiled as he remembered. He looked to Gremble.

"What is your intention for those you send?" Gremble's grin grew.

"Manable and Grisble are both very honorable ogres. They will not allow Elamson to use the ogres as he intends, but they will help him return to the right of his people. They will also help the people of Calisonnos to find the best of lives." Grembo smiled and nodded his approval. "Besides the fact that Morgable is a very strong magical power. He is the one to open the portal for our arrival," Gremble said the last quietly and Grembo's smile grew even wider. "Throw in the fact that Griliana, Grisble's daughter, is a power as well and the fact that she has her eyes on Morgable, it should be quite interesting." Grembo laughed out loud. Grandoa looked to him and then smiled at her mate. She then turned back to those around the table and told them what Gremble had just told his father. They were all soon laughing, except Morgable. He was blushing.

Grrale, named after his great grand sire of the Valley, and leader of the Realm's wolves', with half of the hunting pack, watched the band of Saplese, from his place of concealment. The other half of this hunting pack, being led by his mate, Terryle, watched from the opposite side of the small clearing. Saplese were a much larger Realm version of a rabbit, without the long ears. They had no natural predatory enemies, except the residents of the land. Saplese were a second meat supply, after the herd animals. These creatures could easily get as big as fifty pounds and they were not all that intelligent. Since the arrival of the wolves, eagles and Dragons on the Realm world, there had been a drop in their population, but they had quickly rebounded. It would seem that the three main reasons for Saplese were to eat, breed and be eaten, and they bred faster than rabbits. It was said that a female Saplese could easily birth four litters, of three to five young, a year. It was known that a male would have at least six females in his group. There never seemed to be a shortage of them.

Grrale looked across the field to the eyes of his mate. She gave a small nod of readiness. He returned the nod and then charged. Terryle, and those with her, charged from the other side. The twenty Saplese didn't even have time to start running before the wolves were upon them. The deaths were quick, for as big as the Saplese were, the wolves were much, much, bigger and stronger. They howled the success of the hunt. The wolves, picking the twenty prey up by their backs, began the trip to their central den area. They changed carriers several times before they reached their goal. When they entered the den area, there was a great uproar from the remainder of the pack, for they all would eat well this day.

"Them wolves steal our food Bentarson," Clespian spat at her husband as the faint howls of the wolves successful hunt came to her ears. He didn't even look back at her.

"There are plenty for all Clespian." She glared at him.

"At the next meeting, I am going to suggest that we hunt them wolves and take our food back," she told him in anger. "How long do you think it will take them creatures to start to take our herd animals? And, I fear for the children!" He straightened from the wagon wheel he was repairing and walked to her. The angry look in his eyes caused her to swallow hard.

"You will do no such thing woman. We all asked them wolves, eagles and dragons to come and keep the growth of the Saplese down or don't you remember that our crops were being eaten almost faster than we could plant them. Would you want to go back to standing watches night and day?" Bentarson asked her harshly. "They agreed to leave our stock alone and keep the Saplese in check and they have done that very thing." He looked at her strangely with his next question. "Why would they threaten the children woman? That makes no sense at all. Now tend your work and forget them wolves." He gave her one last hard look and returned to the wheel. She quieted and went back to churning, but she did not forget her desire to rid the area of them wolves.

It had been a week since the arrival of Namson and his family. Namson had been spending most of his time in the company of the Overseer and Mike was very impressed with the boys rapid progress. The rest of his time, he spent with Glornina and everyone was pleased with that. At first, Ventia and Chrystal had had their concerns, but as the week had passed, they had come to know Namson and they were quite satisfied with Glornina's choice. They did admit later though, they really didn't think there was a whole lot they could have done about it even if they had had a problem. Glornina was a very strong willed girl.

Ferlinos sat in the reading room with Renoria and Sen, Vandora's mother and grandmother. They shared tea, with a small amount of brandy added and had been talking of the erupting relationship between Vandora and Gerpinos. Ferlinos thought of her husband, who was out roaming the City Realm and she sighed.

"As much as I agree for the needed marriage of Gerpinos and Vandora, the final decision lies with her father," she said with a degree of concern in her voice. Neither Renoria or Sen missed that concern.

"Why do you think he would object?" Sen asked her. Ferlinos looked to her and almost smiled.

"He doesn't have any idea of what is happening with his daughter," she told them. They both lifted their brows in surprise.

"I don't mean to be disrespectful, but how could he not?" Renoria asked. "They have done everything but mate in the main hall." Ferlinos giggled as she nodded her agreement and Sen glared at her daughter, for her words. Ferlinos looked to the mother of Vandora and smiled. She liked this woman. She was straight from the shoulder and said what she thought and be damned to those who didn't like it. She thought her husband, Crandora, must be a very strong man indeed.

"There is at least one thing you should know of my husband," she told them carefully. She smiled softly as she looked to them. "He is a strong and for the most part, a fair ruler," the other two nodded; "but there are times that he has the tendency to be very self centered and since arriving here in the Realm, he has started to think that he should have more, to be a more powerful ruler."

"Is that why he has enlisted some of the ogres to return to Calisonnos with you?" Sen asked quietly. Ferlinos nodded with a small smile.

"Do not fear, I have talked with those ogres and I think Elamson is not going to like all that comes from that enlistment." Both Sen and Renoria grinned at her.

"Do you think you can sway Elamson about the children?" Sen asked. Ferlinos smiled wider as she looked to Sen.

"Maybe, but it will not be easy with his mind now preoccupied with his desires." She looked to the other two with a slight grin. "I think it would be easier to get him to approve her marriage, without his knowledge of whom the male is." Ventia and Sen looked to each other and then back to her. Ventia began to grin as well. Ferlinos frowned. "I swear, there are times when that man talks, I am sure he thinks with his butt and craps with his mouth." The three laughed loudly with her statement.

———

Cartile, leader of the Realm dragons, his mate Jastile, and their two young, Chartile, their son and his mate Welerlintile. Semitile, Chartile's sister and her mate, Merlintile, were returning to their caves, from a very filling hunt and thinking of a nap. Merlintile was the son of the first mating of a black dragon, Crastamor, and a Realm dragon, Crelintile and was the largest dragon in the Realm. Suddenly, Tremliteen, a faxlie they all knew to be one of the Overseers messengers, flew up beside

Cartile's head, between him and Jastile. Cartile smiled at his small friend. "Tremliteen, to what do I owe this honor? Does not the Overseer keep you busy enough?" Cartile chuckled. Tremliteen joined in his chuckle.

"I am on his business Cartile. He asks that you come to the palace and meet his trainee, if you could." Cartile looked to Jastile. They had just discussed the new trainee that morning and what the father of the boy was attempting with the ogres. Jastile threw up her front claws, in a somewhat shrug and smiled at him. Cartile nodded and returned her smile.

"Very well Tremliteen, you can tell the Overseer we will be there shortly," the dragon said and Tremliteen nodded and shot off, back towards the palace.

"Do you think the father will be there?" Chartile called to his father as they banked their turn back towards the palace.

"Do not worry yourself son and let your father do all the talking," Jastile called to him and it was an order. Chartile glared at her, but Cartile had to grin, for his son had a tendency to try and take over any conversation, no matter who was talking. As they came in to land, on the grass in front of the Palace, Cartile saw Mike and a boy on the front terrace. As he looked to the boy, he was reminded of Mike when he led them all here to the Realm, to battle the forces of Dark Magic. Cartile did not like the appearance of age on his friend. As they landed, Jastile, knowing her son well, landed so as she blocked his way from walking to his father. Chartile tried to get around her and she glared at him. "You are to stay here until your father tells you else wise," she told him. He looked to her and raised to his full height.

"If I am to become leader of the Dragons, I must attend such meetings," he told her in a forceful voice that showed nothing but disrespect to his mother. Cartile, who had heard him, turned completely around and walked back towards his son and he was angry.

"You being the leader of the dragons is not a given thing Chartile," his father stated and his voice showed his anger. The other four, backed from the two. "The one I choose to be leader, will be the one who shows me the most responsibility, intelligence and respect for the dragons and all those of the Realm. The leader I choose will be the one who can demonstrate that responsibility by obeying those who still have the authority to give orders!" Cartile was now nose to nose with his son, even though he had to lower his head to do so, because Chartile was shorter than most dragons. "And if I ever hear you talk to your mother with that tone in your voice again, I guarantee you will not be the leader of the dragons. You will be lucky if you are able to be *walking*, among the dragons!" Cartile was now roaring. Chartile ducked with his fear and backed away. Welerlintile would not go near him, for she was as mad as Cartile and shamed by Chartile's behavior. Semitile and Merlintile glared at him, Merlintile taking a step towards Chartile. Chartile turned his fear and shame into anger, directing it at them, but was smart enough to not say anything, then. It was during this confrontation that Namson leaned to Mike.

"Who is the loud littler one?' he asked as he watched the event.

"Chartile, son of Cartile and Jastile" Mike told him.

"Does he think he is due the leadership of the dragons?" Namson asked further, still watching the dragons.

"He may think it, but if he doesn't get wiser and lose a lot of his arrogance, he won't be," Mike told him and Namson nodded his complete understanding. Cartile turned back to the terrace and tried to calm himself as he neared it.

"My apologies Overseer," he said as he stopped at the steps of the terrace.

"There is no need of apologies between us old friend," Mike told him. Cartile bowed his head slightly. "Cartile, allow me to introduce Namson." Cartile bowed to the lad, which Namson returned. "Namson this is Cartile, my friend, and leader of the dragons of the Realm."

"It is my honor to meet the leader of the dragons of the Realm, for the Overseer has repeatedly spoken of the unmatched talents of all dragons in the battles with the forces of Dark Magic," Namson stated and both Mike and Cartile were surprised by the young man's words.

"I, and all dragons, thank you for your praise Namson," Cartile replied and again bows were shared. "May I present my mate Jastile," Cartile stated and Jastile moved up next to her mate. Namson bowed as did Jastile. "My son Chartile and his mate, Welerlintile." The female moved forward, but Chartile was no longer there. Cartile looked to Welerlintile.

"He walked around the corner and took off. I don't know where he went and I am sorry to do this now, but I must petition to end my joining with him," Welerlintile said with anger in her voice, her colors dimmed with her shame. Jastile moved to her and led her away. Cartile cleared his throat.

"I am sorry to see your troubles lord Cartile. Please let me meet the rest of your family and then perhaps, you should attend to your son," Namson said softly. Cartile nodded.

"My daughter Semitile and her mate, Merlintile." Cartile tried to show the pride he had of them, but his anger was in the way. They bowed and it was answered by Namson and he was surprised to see that Merlintile looked to his eyes steadily. Mike and Namson both felt regret for the events that had happened and they quickly ended the meeting, promising to have another talk at a better time. Cartile thanked them and led his family to his and Jastile cave. He and Jastile comforted Welerlintile and Cartile told her she need not worry about Chartile ever again.

Chartile had flown to the cave of his friend Platile, who was younger. When he arrived, he was met by Straltile, the father of his friend.

"You are not welcome here Chartile," the much larger dragon told him. Chartile looked him in the eyes.

"You would dare talk this way to the soon to be leader of the dragons?" he snarled at Straltile. The older dragon closed in on him.

"You little braggart, you will never be leader of the dragons!" Straltile roared and continued to close on Chartile.

"Platile, the meeting cave," Chartile yelled and dived out of the cave and took off, before Straltile got to him. "Gather the others," was his last order. Straltile turned around and looked to his son.

"You are going nowhere," he roared and pushed the young dragon back into the cave. Several hours later, an angry Platile managed to sneak out and went to gather the other three young males who were part of Chartile's gang. Chartile had flown to his and Welerlintile's cave. He raged when he did not find her there. He made his decision then.

"I am to be the leader of the dragons if I have to kill any who would think to oppose me," he vowed and took off for the meeting cave.

―――――

"That Chartile is going to be trouble," Namson stated as he and Mike reentered the palace. Mike nodded.

"Yes, but unless it spills over onto the lives of others' of the Realm, it is Cartile's to deal with." Namson nodded his understanding.

CHAPTER THREE

It was at the end of the second week of their visitation that Elamson decided that they should return to Calisonnos. The morning of their departure, the ogres who were going with them were waiting just off the front terrace when all walked out. Ferlinos smiled at them and they bowed, a hint of a smile on their faces. Elamson grinned widely as he looked to them, convinced his plans were going perfectly. He turned to the Overseer.

"I am proud that you have chosen my son and I am sure that the decision was the correct one," he told Mike. Mike smiled and nodded.

"I believe you are correct Elamson," Mike told him and glanced at the ogres and they bowed to him. Overseer and ogre grinned as Mike was fully aware of the reasons for their traveling to Calisonnos and what was planned for Elamson's desires. He also knew of the trick the ladies had planned to pull on Elamson and he approved completely. Gerpinos came to her father and gave him a hug. He looked at her confused as she went to her mother. Mike and the others' hid their smiles from the Ruler of Calisonnos.

"What is this?" he asked both daughter and wife. Ferlinos looked at him wide eyed.

"Do you not want your daughter to make the best wife for her husband? she asked him. He nodded.

"Of course, but what is happening. Gerpinos is coming, right?" he asked without conviction. Ferlinos shook her head.

"She is going to stay a while longer and learn all she can here," she told her husband, while Ventia, Renoria, Heather, Chrystal, Sen, and Gerpinos, fought with all their might not to laugh out loud. "That way, when she returns to Calisonnos, she will be a very wise wife. You do want your daughter to wed do you not?" she asked hurrying her words.

"Of course I want her to wed, but . . . ." Elamson tried to speak.

"Well, this is the best way to ensure that is what happens! Now, can we go?" she asked Elamson and looked to Mike with a wink. Mike realized that Elamson had no idea he had just given his approval for Gerpinos to marry and he had no idea to whom. Gerpinos gave her mother a long hug. "Be happy and teach him all you can about Calisonnos, for when you bring him to Calisonnos, your father is not going to be easy to live with for a while," she whispered to her daughter and Gerpinos giggled her understanding. Ferlinos turned to Elamson, giving him a exasperated, impatient look. Elamson waved to all and opened the portal, as Ferlinos winked at Ventia, Renoria, Heather, Chrystal and Sen. The two parents, followed by the grinning ogres passed through and the portal closed. Ventia turned to Mike.

"Now, let's get them married," she said, glancing to Gerpinos and Vandora.

"Please," Renoria added with feeling. Mike laughed and turned to the young lovers.

"Do you both accept the responsibility of the marriage you ask for?" he asked them. They both smiled. "We do," they said together. Mike nodded and handed Gerpinos a parchment. "You are now husband and wife," he told them. Gerpinos grabbed the parchment as Vandora picked her up and carrying her, ran into the palace.

"I hope they make it all the way to their room," Namson said softly, putting his arm around Glornina and everyone started to laugh rather loudly as they followed, at much slower pace, into the palace. Namson and Glornina were wed the next day and there was a great celebration for both young couples.

As time moved determinately, Castope's plans had been developing, but there was something she had learned that put a momentary hold on them. "Mistress, we cannot wait, the time is right," Ralsanac stated, fully aware of

Castope's plans. Castope looked to him and she made no attempt to hide the irritation in her eyes.

"I told you Ralsanac, we wait until the death of the Overseer and then we strike. They will be in mourning and the young, who are not experienced in warfare will be unprepared and easy pickings," she told him.

"Mistress," he tried one more time. "There are still many who were involved in the battles with Palakrine. If we wait, how much are they going to teach those who are to be easy pickings?" Castope glared at him. He held her eyes for a moment, hoping she did not see through his false urgings.

"Watch your words Ralsanac," she spat at him. He bowed and held that position. She rose from her chair and came from behind her desk. Her eyes locked on the form of Ralsanac. "There is something much more important than my plans for the Realm at this time," she told her Dremlorian advisor. He lifted his head and looked into her eyes and he trembled at the rage he saw there. *What has she learned*, he worried. "It would seem that my oldest daughter and her elfin sire are plotting against me," she whispered her anger. Ralsanac waited on her words as Castope opened her door and looked to the guard there. "Bring Prateope to me, now," she ordered. The guard bowed and hurried to the youngest daughters quarters. Castope turned to Ralsanac and an evil smile came to her lips. "Do you know how I learned of this thing?" she asked him as she returned to her desk and chair. Ralsanac slowly shook his head as Prateope entered the room. She walked to her mother and into her arms. Castope looked to Ralsanac and smiled even wider. "She told me." Prateope looked to him and her grin was even more evil than her mother's. "She told me of her older sisters defection from me. She told me because she hates her sister for that desertion." Ralsanac tried, but failed to stop the tremor that traveled through him. Castope rose from her chair and took Prateope's hand. "Come, it is time to stop the treachery of my oldest daughter and the elf." She led the way from the room and passed the squad of soldiers and a doctor, who waited in the hallway. In just a few minutes she stopped in front of a section of wall, on the first floor below ground level. She smiled at Ralsanac and blasted a hole in the wall, that had been a door.

The guards charged into the room, followed by Castope, Prateope, the doctor and then Ralsanac. The guards immediately grabbed Morsalon and Cartope's arms, pinning them. The others in the room were herded to one corner. No one saw that Ragella had knelt down, in the back of the pack. She placed her hands to her head, her eyes closed, and began sending to the strongest receivers in the Domains of the Rightful Magic. Castope smiled gently as she went to her oldest daughter, pulling the doctor with her. She looked deeply into her daughters eyes when she stopped and pulled the doctor to the girl. "Is she ready yet?" she asked and the doctor placed his hand on the girls lower abdomen. He stood for a moment and then turned his head to Castope.

"Not yet Mistress, but it will not be long and she will be ready to breed," the doctor said and Cartope glared into her mother's eyes, for all knew of her mother's intention to mate her to a Demon. Castope looked to the two guards that held the girl.

"Take her to cell number one, in my quarters," she told them and they took the struggling girl from the room. Prateope suddenly cried out and pushed her way into the huddled group in the corner. "What?" Castope asked.

"Ragella sends a message to the Domains," the girl cried out. Castope lunged forward and opened the passage wider. When she broke through, she saw her seer kneeling and holding her head with her eyes closed. Ragella kept sending until her body splattered against the wall behind her, from the force of the blast spell Castope hit her with. All turned their heads from the gore that had been the sorceress. Castope turned and approached Morsalon. A smile returned to her lips as she stopped in front of him.

"I will decide how you are to die, after you have witnessed the taking of your daughter by many, many, Demons," she hissed at him. "Take him to the other cell in my quarters," she told the guards who held him. She turned to the frightened eyes of the others' in the room without a smile. She turned around and started to leave. When she got to Ralsanac, she gave him his instructions. "Destroy them all," she ordered and left the room with a grinning Prateope. Ralsanac looked over all those before him. He sighed and lifted his hands. To the guards who were left to witness the slaughter, it appeared as though Ralsanac did indeed kill all, but in actuality, he put them into a deep coma. A coma he could wake them from later. He did this because he was the aide of the leaders of the rebellion against Castope and he knew he would need these people later. The problem he now had was, that those two leaders had just been led from the room under guard and had to be saved, somehow!

Two of Somora's spies, that were to report on Castope's actions, raced for another secret meeting room. They knew that Somora's sensing's would soon come to pass

Heather, Glornina and most all of those who were seers or talkers, heard the frantic and detailed sending of Ragella. They were all very surprised, as was Mike, that Namson had heard it as well. It was then that the young man took over as Overseer, though Mike would not yield official control for another year. As the talks of what must be done were begun, Mike stayed more to the back ground, allowing Namson to take the lead and make the decisions, with his supervision.

Jardan, without lifting his head, looked to his wife. Dana stirred the bowl of soup with the absence of any knowledge of doing so. His nephew, Quoslon, who was the son of his younger sister Narisha, and had come to the North West Domain at her request, to assume the position of Keeper of Magic, because of Jardan's age and failing heath, watched his aunt as well. Xanalenor, Quoslon's wife, took Quoslon's arm, for she worried for Dana as well as all those of the Domains.

"Dana?" she asked tentatively. "What are your thoughts?" The woman looked to her and it took a moment for her to return to their world. She blushed and looked to her husband, nephew, his wife and their son, Edward.

"I'm sorry," she told them. She straightened her shoulders and looked to each of them again, trying to smile.

"What is it honey?" Jardan asked softly, as he struggled to his feet. She looked to him and her eyes began to fill with tears. Jardan came to her and put his arms around her as Xanalenor tightened her grip on Quoslon's arm. Dana put her face into his neck.

"When will it stop?" she cried her question softly. Jardan pulled his wife to him, even tighter.

"I don't know Dana, but until it does, we must fight it," Jardan told her softly. Her head nodded with the truth, but her tears told of her feelings. The same feelings were shared by many throughout the Domains. Jardan and Quoslon exchanged looks. Both nodded slightly. Quoslon then looked to his son, Edward. The young man rose and went to an orb and contacted Namson, to find out what was to be done.

―――⚬⚬⚬⚬⚬⚬―――

Trolls were the shortest of all the creatures of the magical Domains, with the exception of the Fairy Folk, at an average height of four feet tall. That did not mean that they were the weakest, or the quietest! Their broad shoulders and powerful hands, easily showed all that they possessed great strength. The males all carried very large mallets and they knew how to use them for many different things! "I doooo nooooot like the new way they act!" Porsel roared as he talked with Zardan, upset over the manner of production of new Milky Crystal amulets design. He was glaring at Ponsel, who stood beside the troll leader. "They doooo nooooot doooo as we did or they shoooould!" Zardan sighed, or the troll equivalent.

"Poooorsel, that is the way they doooo it!" Zardan told his second in command, about the younger trolls at the mines. "We accepted their ways when we foooought Palakrine. Noooow we are toooo accept their ways again. The Ooooverseer has soooo coooomanded!" Zardan said with his authority as clan leader. Porsel glared at him for a moment and then turned and stomped off. Zardan sighed again, looked to Ponsel and then the two continued on to the Overseers palace.

———

The two trolls arrived at the gate and were told to enter right away. They were surprised, but went into the palace and were met by Pelkraen, the lead Meleret of the palace. He led them to Mike's office and they both were even more surprised to see Namson sitting behind the desk and Mike sitting in front of it. Mike smiled at their widened eyes.

"He is in charge, with my support," he told them simply. They nodded, glancing at the young man. Zardan turned to Ponsel.

"Alright, repooooort yooooourself," he commanded the younger troll. Ponsel looked to Namson and then Mike several times and then finally spoke.

"We have goooot yooooour message and we prepare foooor the needs yoooou ask foooor," he told the two at the desk, still not sure which one he should really be telling. Namson nodded and smiled at Mike and then the trolls.

"Thank you, I wasn't sure you would understand what I wanted." Namson told the younger troll. Zardan looked to Mike.

"This is noooot what we did befoooore. There are many questiooooon." Mike nodded and looked to Namson.

"Go ahead, tell them," he told Namson. The young Overseer nodded and looked to Zardan.

"This time, we are not going to let the users of Dark Magic pick the time of attack," Namson said as he leaned forward in his chair, placing his forearms on the desk, his hands clasped. "We are going to attack them!" Zardan's eyes opened wide as Ponsel smiled.

"Ya, goooood," Ponsel stated in a loud voice. Zardan still looked to Mike.

"Is this soooo?" he asked quietly, as much as a troll could be quiet about anything. Mike nodded, a grin coming to his lips.

"We will be ready!" Ponsel roared. Namson smiled at the troll.

"I will come by the mines soon and check on what you have done," he told Ponsel and the troll nodded, turned and left the palace, leaving Zardan staring at Mike. Mike could not help the chuckle that came to him.

"He has a very good basic idea and I agree. We can't wait this time. This leader of the Dark Forces has more power than we have faced before. We have to surprise them, and hard," he told the leader of the troll clan. Zardan didn't move his head as his eyes shifted slowly to Namson. Namson laughed out loud.

———

Maelie, Brei, Renoria and Glory, who was Heather and Tyrus's youngest and had wed Paul, Jenny and Davian's youngest, were walking the grounds around the Corsendorian castle. The sun shone brightly and the birds were singing. Maelie looked to where the nannies fought, not always quietly, over the care of children and grandchildren.

"I'm worried," Glory said softly. Brei gave a gentle chuckle.

"Is that all?" she asked. "I'm scared half crazy."

"Only half," Renoria asked with a short chuckle of her own.

"Namson has the beginnings of a good plan and the Overseer is behind him." Maelie said as a sigh. "I'm not sure how high the price is going to be, but we have a better chance this way than waiting for them to decide the time and way." Her voice was calm and quiet, but the rest heard the dread of what they, and all of all Domains, felt in their hearts. The other three exchanged quick glances and then looked to the children who were trying the patience of the best of nannies. Most of the children were already old enough to tend to themselves, but the rule of the land said that they needed supervision, so the nannies fought on valiantly.

━━━━━━⟡━━━━━━

From one of the windows of his office, King Cranedoran watched the four women below, as they talked. Queen Xanaloren came quietly to his side. "Our sons tell me that the ideas of the new Overseer is good and that we should support him completely," she told him as she too looked to those outside. Her husband sighed, loudly. She looked to him and gently took his hand. "I know how you feel about wars, but I think Crendosa and Crondasa are right this time. We have always stayed separate from the wars, but we need to stand with our allies this time." He looked to her and she did not waver from his eyes. He sighed again and turned from the window and returned to his desk. She did not follow, but watched him as he sat.

"What worries me my love, is that I agree with you and our sons," he told her simply, returning her look, as a small grin came to his lips. "I just wish I knew what to do about it, especially, how to prepare," he sighed his words.

He then straightened his shoulders and looked to her seriously. "I had better alert Caldora of our decision." The King called for a messenger, to alert the General of their meager armies.

"My love," Xanaloren said. "I believe that our grandson, Crandora is in communication with the new Overseer and is keeping Crendosa well informed." Cranedoran nodded as the messenger arrived. General Caldora was shocked when he received the message from his King. Until this time, his entire experience with the military had been ceremonial. He went straight to Prince Crendosa and asked what he was to do. The prince smiled and began to tell him what was needed to be done. Caldora hoped the Prince did not see him begin to tremble, when he received his instructions. The Prince did see his reaction to the directions and realized that Caldora was not prepared to deal with what was to be. Prince Crendosa then took command of the armies. After telling his father of his decision, he began to plan his building and training, of the Corsendorian army.

"What do you mean, you won't?" Elamson yelled at Grisble. The ogre developed a less than happy expression, as did Morgable, who stood with him and Elamson quickly rethought his approach. "I thought I made my meaning clear to you when I invited you to come here," Elamson said in a very controlled voice. Grisble smiled and nodded.

"You did, but after being with the people of Calisonnos, and a lot of thought and time, we ogres have realized that it would be wrong to do as you desire," Grisble said. Elamson started to lose his temper.

"If you do not do what I want, you are of no use to me and I will send you back whence you came," he tried to growl at the much larger ogre. Grisble's smile held as he slowly shook his head.

"I do not think that you will," Grisble said quietly, for an ogre. "We have many friends here now and I do not think you want them as enemies, especially with you trying to change the just laws your father had set in place and all have lived by since." Elamson's face began to redden as his temper built.

"I rule Calisonnos now!" Elamson roared and was obviously not thinking when he took a step closer to the much larger ogre. "I invited you and I can return you." Grisble placed a finger against Elamson's chest and stopped his forward momentum. Morgable, even bigger than Grisble, stepped closer and to the side of Elamson.

"I think it best that you remember what you had announced to all, when we arrived," Grisble said, his voice still very calm.

"That we were welcome to stay as long as, *we*, wanted," Morgable, having to bend to whisper in Elamson's ear. "Do you really think your people would like the fact that you did not mean your words and, that you only brought us here to help force them to be slaves?"

"I truly believe that you would have many more problems if that news were to be revealed, don't you?" Grisble added. Elamson's face, still red with anger, started to show another look. The look of doubt. "I think it best that you reconsider your efforts, don't you?" Grisble had not lost his smile.

"And," Ferlinos said coming through the door; "change the new laws you are trying to impose, back to the ways that were before!" Elamson glared at her, his anger returning. She glared back. "Don't give me that look," she told him and then her voice turned only slightly softer. "Do you really want me to talk to the people about your true purpose of bringing the ogres here?" His eyes opened wide in spite of his anger. "How many do you think would believe me over anything you might say after." She smiled slightly with her words. Elamson actually started to growl and his fists clenched. Ferlinos looked to him with saddened eyes. "You were a fair and good leader before you went to the Realm, but you started to forget that point when you saw what was there. You started to think yourself more than you should be." She touched his cheek softly. "Please come back to me my husband and come back to your people." He stared at her for several minutes before the red of his face began to fade. He turned to Grisble. The ogre nodded and waited. Elamson turned and went to the large window and looked out on the city that was the capital of all the Domain. He saw that most of the people glared at the Capital building as they passed and there were some who looked with fear. There were some that looked with sadness. He slowly started to understand what he had done. He had let the thought of power and control, try to take the value of the people of Calisonnos, away from them. He turned around and walked around the three who watched him and out of the door of his office. He went straight to Minister Monason's office and opened the door. Without entering he gave his order.

"Monason, retract any laws I have ordered to be, since my return from the Realm. We will live with the laws of before!" He slammed the door, cutting off the sigh of relief from the Minister and returned to his office. He went to his desk and sat down. He glanced at the three who still watched him. "What are you three waiting for, I have work to do," he told them and picked up a stack of parchments and started to go through them. Ferlinos smiled at him and turned to the ogres.

"Could you show the beer makers again, how your brew is made?" she asked as they turned to the door. "Elamson and many of Calisonnos have taken a liking to it." Grisble and Morgable grinned as they nodded and followed her out of the door. Two weeks later, Vandora and Gerpinos arrived in Calisonnos and Elamson faced a new trial. One he was again shown he must accept. In a short time though, he found that Vandora had a powerful talent to command and a daughter who supported him with a ferocity that was frightening!

———◦◦◦◦◦◦◦———

Heather looked to the young men gathered on the rear terrace. Edward, son of Quoslon, representing the North West Domain. Crandon, the grandson of Crondasa and Brie, representing the South West. Prestilon, son of Sonilon, the North East and Norson, grandson of Matsar, the South East. Semotor, grandson of Roulitor, representing Ventoria. Jarsalon, son of Jardilan, who was the son of Dana and had taken over as Keeper of magic of Dolaris at his mother's request when her mother Katie, had died, representing Dolaris. Croldena, grandson of Crendosa and Maelie, representing Corsendora and Vandora, representing Calisonnos, all sat huddled in silent talk. Tyrus came to her side and put his arm around her lovingly.

"They plan," she told him. He nodded. "Why can't I hear them?" she asked fearfully. He chuckled.

"As our parents could not hear us, we cannot hear them," he told her. She sighed.

"My father was part of our plans," she answered. He sighed softly.

"Not until you included him my dear," he told her. She glanced at him and her eyes were hard. He returned her look with the eyes of age and truth. She finally saw his truth and turned back to the ones on the terrace. Namson and Glornina suddenly appeared and joined the gathered. Heather watched the silent discussion with tears forming. *They are going to do what they must*, Heather thought to herself.

"He will lead them as he should and must, but why are we being kept out?" she asked herself out loud.

"As Maltakrine was your fathers battle, and Palakrine and Saltakrine was yours and your brothers, this is his," he answered. He felt her shudder. The mates of those already there started to appear and the coordinating took on a whole new level.

"I still miss his presence," she said through her increased tears of missing.

"I know my love, I know," he answered and she turned to him, coming into his arms.

"I pray for them, and us," she said into his chest.

"So do I my love, so do I." he told her softly.

"I'm tired of them wolves, eagles and Dragons taking our food!" Clespian screamed out as she suddenly jumped to her feet. The entire council meeting silenced at her outburst. Bentarson grabbed her hand and yanked her back to her seat.

"I told you woman, them wolves have lived by their agreement and there's plenty for everyone!" he roared. She yanked her hand from his and stood again.

"You've all seen them critters, in the air and on the ground, circling your lands and homes. Do you think they are just looking for Saplese? Nah, they looking for prey and they circle our herds, and our children!" Bentarson grabbed her hand again and pulled her back down. There were several women in the council room that looked to their husbands with very worried looks.

"Now you hush woman," he yelled at her. "Them critters have all obeyed the agreement and you got no cause to try to stir things this way."

"I won't be quiet Bentarson! I was quiet the last two meetings, but I'm not going to be quiet this time," she screamed at him. "You men say something and you don't got the brains of a Saplese about a mothers fears." The rock, used to get attention by the council leader, began to pound on the table.

"Bentarson," the council leader yelled. "If you can't control her, get her out of here and we will think about if she is to come back."

"That's because us men think about the truth of things and not the foolish fears of what abouts," Bentarson hollered at her and yanked her to her feet. "Now see what you done with your foolishness, we gotta leave and I haven't heard the totals on our produce yet!"

"You aren't going to care about no produce totals when them critters tear into our home and eat us one night!" she screamed as she was pulled from the building. More of the women and a few men, with smaller farms and single, looked worried. Bentarson put his wife in the back of the wagon, none to gently, and climbed to the seat. Grabbing the reins he got the six legged draft animals moving, cussing to himself about his wife, and women in general. Because of the noise of the animals pulling the wagon, the wagon itself, and his own mumblings, he didn't feel or hear his wife as she slid from the wagon and reentered the council building, screaming all kinds of things. Nor did he hear the outcry of a man who entered from the other side of the building, claiming that a dragon had just taken his best stock breeder, nor the other two that came into the meeting, screaming the same thing. Bentarson didn't realize that Clespian was gone until he stopped to water the animals at the creek, three miles away. By then it was much, much, too late to do anything about it. His anger became confusion when he returned to his farm and his oldest son told him that a dragon had taken one of the best of the stock herd!

Heather stood between Cartile and Jastile. A mere shadow of a figure, so overwhelmed by the size of the dragons that flanked her. She lifted her hands and the portal opened. Through it came the two newest members of the dragons of the Realm, Hanatile and Nalatile. As soon as they had cleared the portal and Heather had let it close, they bowed to the two who were considered by all of the Plains dragons, especially Dartile, the younger brother of Cartile and the designated heir for the leadership of the Plain dragons, as the greatest of dragons, Cartile and Jastile. They looked to Heather and bowed to her as well. She returned their bow.

"Welcome to the Realm," she told them and turned to Cartile. "I must return to the palace, I don't want to be too far from daddy for too long," she told him and he nodded his understanding. She reached out her hand

and touched Jastile and the dragon gently nuzzled her cheek. Heather smiled at her and then the two new ones and disappeared. Even though the two had seen the appearance and disappearance of others' in the Plain, they still twitched at Heather's sudden departure. Cartile chuckled.

"You will get used to the appearance and disappearance of the Overseer's family and the leaders of the Domains, for they are all very strong in Magic," he told the recently paired couple. "Jastile will show you the vacant caves and you can pick the one you want. She will also give you a quick tour of the Realm, by air." The two rather wide eyed young dragons nodded with hesitation. "In a couple of days, after you have had a chance to settle and meet the other dragons of the Realm, we will talk," he told them and gave Jastile a short neck caress and leapt into the air and flew off. They looked to Jastile with confused expressions. She tried to smile.

"Who was the woman?" Nalatile asked.

"She is the one called Heather, the Overseer's daughter and the sister of the one called Zachia, who had been killed." Jastile told her. The two nodded, for these names were familiar to them. The image of the woman stayed with Nalatile. She would remember the look of sadness she had seen in her eyes and later, it would give her the strength and purpose to do something she never thought she could do.

"Does Lord Cartile have other business?" Hanatile asked with care, as not to offend. Jastile nodded her head once and looked to the ground for a second and then lifted her head.

"Yes, he searches for our rebellious son, for he has been causing problems and he needs to be stopped," Jastile told them. "If you are ready, follow me to the caves," she said and leapt into the air. They quickly glanced to each other and then followed.

Renless and Persetine exited the permanent portal that Quansloe had reestablished and began their search for Dereress and Peantine, the leader of the Plains unicorn herd and his mate. They asked the first unicorn they came to and found out that the ones they sought were in the court yard of the castle, with Quansloe. They thanked the unicorn and started for the castle.

"Do you think we should just walk in on them?" Persetine asked. Renless chuckled.

"What effects the Plain, affects the Valley," he told her gently. "We should know what the Keeper plans as much as Dereress," he added as they entered the gate.

"Renless," Quansloe called out; "I am so glad you have shown up. Hello Persetine, it is good to see you as well." The two from the Valley stopped near Dereress and Peantine. The four exchanged the formal bows and then the mares shared a neck rubbing. "We had just started, please join us," Quansloe said.

"We would be honored Keeper," Renless stated with a nod to Dereress.

"As I started to explain to Dereress and Peantine, whatever the plans Namson and the Overseer are making, I am not sure they are thinking of the chance of a retaliatory attack on the Plain, but I do not think it would be unwise to prepare for one anyway." Both lead stallions nodded their agreement. "Nothing definite has been decided, so I want you both to try and think of what your herds could do if that event did happen. I've talked with all the races of Plain and Valley about this and have set the same challenge to them." Again the stallions nodded. Quansloe shrugged at them. "That's about all I have now. Let me know what you can come up with, okay?"

"So much for finding the peace of the Valley and the joy of life there," Persetine muttered to Renless. She referred to what DeeDee had recommended to Renless and her, prior to her death. Dereress and Peantine looked to her in confusion.

Cartile and Merlintile stood on the knoll, waiting for the called fathers of Chartile's gang members. The first to arrive was Straltile, father of Platile. As soon as the dragon father had landed, both Cartile and Merlintile could see the enraged pulsing of his colors. Straltile walked to the leader of the dragons.

"What you do with Chartile is yours to do, but I will deal with Platile myself," he told Cartile. Cartile simply nodded his understanding as the other fathers landed. When they had all gathered, Cartile told them of what they must do.

"These five have attacked and carried off four herd stock of Realm citizens and have broken the agreement that had been formed with those citizens," he stated. All shook their heads, their colors dimming with shame and disbelief that their sons would cause this breach of dragon truth. "We must find them and stop this wanton violation of dragon vows." They all nodded, their colors brightening with their anger. "Have any of you heard your sons talk of this meeting cave?" Cartile looked from one to the next.

"I have," Worslitile said and stepped forward. "It is somewhere in the mountains to the north east, but that is all I know," he told Cartile. The leader of the dragons nodded.

"There are six faxlies coming and we shall split, each with a faxlie. The one who finds this cave will alert the rest of us." There were nods from all. The six faxlies arrived and the six dragons took flight towards the north eastern mountains. It took most of the morning for them to locate the cave and the five who had violated the dignity of all dragons. It was Merlintile who found it and he sent his faxlie to notify the others'. He watched the cave and waited for the fathers to arrive. He could hear the voices of the five, but mostly he heard the voice of Chartile, rousing his followers to a new fervor of excitement, to do more damage to the citizens and this time he meant to attack the citizens themselves!

"I shall drive the good name of Cartile into the dirt with these violations of the agreement that Cartile formed with the weakling humans of the Realm and none shall ever trust him again. Then I shall be the voice that leads the dragons of the Realm!" he screamed to his followers and they roared their support, just as Cartile and the others landed besides Merlintile. Cartile fought the rage that would take him and told the fathers his plan. They all nodded their agreement and moved to the places Cartile had designated. When all were in place, Cartile and Merlintile stepped into the clearing in front of the cave that held the rebels.

"Chartile, come out and face me!" Cartile roared at the entrance of the cave. There was a few seconds of hushed whispering from the cave and then Chartile led the other four out to face his father. When they had landed, Chartile sneered at Merlintile.

"I could have expected you to be here, trying to place yourself in the good eye of the soon to be ousted leader of the dragons. It will do you no good Merlintile, for I shall be leader soon and I will make sure you are dealt with properly!"

"Shut up Chartile!" Cartile roared and Chartile flinched from the roar, but quickly recovered, bolstered by the four that backed him, though some of them did not look all that sure now. "You have damaged the dignity of all dragons with your foolish and greedy behavior." Cartile growled as he slowly advanced on his son.

"You are no longer going to be respected father and I shall lead those who are willing to face a new roll for the dragons of the Realm." Chartile tried his bluster at Cartile. Cartile gave a nod and the fathers came from their places of concealment and the six formed a ring around the young five. Several of the young immediately took a submissive posture. "I will lead the Realm Dragons!" Chartile roared and flamed his father. Cartile charged, ducking, and the flames went harmlessly down his back. Cartile turned his head and closed his jaws on Chartile's neck, just below his head and gave a vicious twist. Chartile's neck snapped loud enough for all to hear. His lifeless body fell as Cartile released his neck. No sound was heard as the young looked to the body of Chartile. They lifted their eyes to Cartile and they saw, and felt, his anger. Cartile raised his head to full height and looked to the four remaining.

"I will leave your punishments to your fathers and I shall be watching each of you in the future." Cartile looked to the four fathers. "Merlintile and I will gather Grrale, the leader of the wolves and Vralar, the leader of the eagles and try to repair the damage that these whelps have caused." With that said, Cartile and Merlintile leapt into the air. Once they had contacted the wolf and eagle, they went to Namson, to try and arrange a meeting with the Realm citizens. Namson, it turned out, was a very good negotiator and Bentarson and Clespian, who had lost stock as well as the other three human families, got Platile to work for them for a year.

At the cave, the four fathers looked to their sons and each of the sons began to tremble with fear. All fathers had previously agreed that as part of their punishment, their sons must serve a year as slaves to the farmers who had lost stock to the rebels, but first, they were going to receive a proper chastisement. The fathers moved in as the young sons cowered. Afterwards, in their pain, they were required to take Chartile's body farther into the mountains and bury it and none were allowed near the site, ever!

CHAPTER FOUR

The morning sun had just cleared the horizon, as the representatives, who had attended the first impromptu meeting in the North East Domain, gathered again, in the Overseers office, for a real purpose. They were all surprised that Mike was not in attendance, until Namson explained that he wanted their ideas to be brought out without the intimidations of the Overseers eyes, and judgments. Namson could see in their eyes that some of them were concerned, at first, that perhaps Namson was trying to take over the role of Overseer too soon. Namson and Glornina exchanged small grins.

"The reason that I wanted your ideas in this manner, was to insure that fresh ideas could be discussed without the worries of traditional thinking's," he said. "We are the ones who will have to do this and we all must be sure that the way we have decided, to accomplish what we must, is what we all are comfortable with. We are not trying to exclude anyone, just trying to find our own way to do what we must." He looked to all who had gathered, one by one. There were a few minutes of exchanged looks among them and then Vandora looked to Namson.

"What do you plan Namson?" he asked calmly. Namson and Glornina exchanged looks, again, and Namson placed his forearms on the desk, his hands clasped, and Glornina sat on the arm of his chair, her hand resting on his shoulder.

"I do not think that we can wait for the Dark Forces to pick the time and way they are going to attack. We must attack them first, to beat them before they can finish their plots. So, the first thing we need to do is get into this Dark City and find out what we face there," he told them. There were nodded heads throughout the group.

"That is why Vandora," Glornina said, with a grin; "Namson and I would like you to ask that your sister Pelinoria, join us in our planning." Vandora's eyes brows barely fluttered with surprise before a grin came to his lips and he nodded as he looked to Crandon and Pentilian.

"Why would you ask that?" Jarsalon asked and his wife, Quentoria, slapped his arm, with a look of disbelief in her eyes.

"Because," Vandora answered, his grin growing, as did Pentilian's and Crandon's; "my little sister, and Pentilian, have both inherited our grandfather Zachia's ability of invisibility, that cannot be sensed." There were a few, who already knew this fact, including Glornina and Namson, who joined Pentilian's and Crandon's chuckles. The rest just looked to Pentilian with lifted brows. Vandora looked to Carla, the strongest talker after Heather.

"You didn't know that?" Quentoria asked Jarsalon in a whisper that all heard, and that added to the chuckling.

"Would you please?" he asked quietly. Carla nodded, her grin wide, and called to Pelinoria, in Olistown, where she lived with her husband Morgan. She looked to Vandora and nodded. Vandora moved his hand slightly, with whispered words and Pelinoria and Morgan, stood in the office, grinning at everyone.

The two quickly found extra chairs and sat, Pelinoria and Pentilian sitting side by side. The cousins took each others' hand as Namson began to outline what he wanted of them. "All right, is there anyone who didn't hear Regella's message from the Dark City?" he asked, looking around the room. There were exchanged looks and each was very serious. "Okay, we learned a general description of the layout of the city from that, but we need a more detailed understanding." Heads nodded around the room. "Pelinoria, Pentilian, I want you two to start at the very outside, eastern edge of the city and work your way into it." Both young woman nodded. "Go slow and carefully. I need you to look for the strengths of the buildings." Again the women nodded. "We need to know the street patterns and if there are any kind of fortifications around the city." Again there were nods. "This is the first of your missions, so don't try to do everything. Start slow, learn it completely and then return and we will start our maps." They both nodded again and turned to their husband. They kissed them and then stood, side by side, holding hands. "Carefully," Namson told them with emphases. They nodded and disappeared. There was silence as all thought of what was happening and what their futures might be. Namson stood. "There's nothing else we can do for now, so why don't we all gather in the reading room for coffee and try to figure out some sort of pattern to work our plans, while we wait on Pentilian and Pelinoria to return," he told them all. There were voices of agreement and ideas as they all stood. Glornina asked a Meleret to bring coffee and tea to the reading room and they all migrated there.

Mike and Palysee were coming out of the dining room, heading for Mike's office, just in time to see the group entering the reading room. "They begin their planning in earnest; they begin their planning in earnest," Palysee sang in a whisper. Mike nodded as he led them to the office. There was a mixture of pride and worry in his eyes.

Pentilian and Pelinoria appeared, invisibly, on the far eastern side of the city, out passed the dragons cave. Ever since they were very young, they had worked on their invisibility talents and had adjusted it so they could see each other, as shadows, and still not be seen or sensed by anyone else. They had also worked out a series of hand signals so they could talk to each other. They didn't want to use their minds to talk because that could be detected by another talker that was close. They were still holding hands as they look around the land before them. Pentilian pointed out the caves and both studied them and their relative position to the city proper. They watched for a while, remembering the comings and goings of the dragons. When they both had a clear picture in their minds, they separated by twenty feet and moved slowly towards the city. They would stop every so often to study the layouts they were seeing. They spent the hours of the morning memorizing everything they could see. The sun was at its highest when they returned to the Realm, appearing in the reading room. Namson made a small stack of large paper to appear in front of both women and each began drawing what they had seen, telling all there, their opinions as they drew. Lunch was brought to them as they all discussed what the women had seen and the maps they had drawn.

Cartile, since the death of his son, had taken to staying to his and Jastile's cave more and more. He had done what had needed to be done, and he knew that, but to have to have been the one to do it, affected him more than he wanted to admit. With the word that Namson and the representatives of the other Domains were beginning their planning's, he knew that there needed to be a dragon to lead the dragon forces in the coming conflicts. Jastile was surprised and worried, when he rose early that morning and left their cave, without a word to her. "Merlintile, could I have a word with you?" Cartile asked from the entrance of Merlintile's and Semitile's cave. The two exchanged surprised looks and Merlintile walked to the cave entrance.

"Yes Cartile, what is it?" he asked, stopping in front of the dragon leader.

"Fly with me," Cartile said and leapt into the air. Merlintile glanced over his shoulder at Semitile and saw the worry in her eyes.

"I will be right back," he told her and followed Cartile, to the west. The two flew for several minutes, landing on the shore of a rather large lake. Cartile led them to an open area and turned to face his daughters mate. Merlintile could not help but see the turmoil in Cartile's eyes. "What is it?" Merlintile asked, keeping his voice calm. Cartile sighed.

"There is a battle coming, and the dragons will be part of it," he said quietly, looking intently into the younger and larger Merlintile's eyes. "I would ask that you take command of the dragons that are to be part of that battle." There was silence for a moment, before Merlintile replied.

"I of course, would be honored to do so," he said; "but as dragon leader, shouldn't you do that?" he asked, trying to keep his concerns for the well being of Cartile from his voice. The dragon leader sighed again, but it was softer.

"I have seen the friendship that is growing between you and the new Overseer," Cartile said, but his voice did not carry the familiar tone of authority. Merlintile's concerns grew stronger. "Namson's thoughts are not going to be as I am used to and I think that you would be better able to adjust to his ideas at this time. Plus, many of the younger dragons, that will be joining this crusade, would be very willing to follow your lead." Merlintile watched Cartile as he spoke and he did not like the tiredness he could now see in the dragon leaders eyes.

"Cartile," Merlintile said softly; "what was done with Chartile, was what was needed to be done. You should not blame yourself for Chartile's wrongful ways." Cartile nodded slightly.

"I know that Merlintile, and I thank you for your support, but I need you to do this now. I will work with those of the Realm, in case there is need for defense here." Cartile's voice seemed stronger with these words. A moment or two passed and then Merlintile nodded.

"Very well Cartile, I will do what you ask of me," Merlintile said, with a bow. Cartile bowed and the two leapt into the air and returned to their caves. They told their mates what had been decided. Semitile was very concerned about her father and later met with her mother about it. The two females agreed that Cartile was hurting, but they both knew that Jastile, and the Overseer, were the only ones who could help the dragon leader through this. Semitile returned to her mate and Jastile went to the palace, and the Overseer.

Besonlor tried to be patient as she watched the King talking with those who had petitioned for this time. She had been listening to Heather, and the other talkers of the Domains, and she knew that King Martoran would want to know what was happening in the Realm and what was now thought another threat to all Domains.

"Besonlor, you look like your waiting in line for cake and are afraid they're going to run out before you get any," Queen Restone said quietly as she stopped next to the most powerful talker in all of Belthume. Besonlor had jumped when the Queen had first spoken, but now gave her bow and a strained smile. The Queen tensed for the look on Besonlor's face. "What is it Besonlor?" she asked, her voice even more hushed than before. Besonlor glanced to the King, who was now looking to her and the Queen.

"There is another threat of Dark Magic, to the Realm and the Domains of Rightful Magic," she whispered. The Queen's eyes opened wide and she looked to the King. Martoran, King of Belthume, quickly ended the session with the store owner who was truly wasting his time and came towards the two. When near, Restone spoke before the King could ask.

"Besonlor says that there is another threat of Dark Magic to the Realm and Domains," she told her husband. Martoran looked to the talker.

"What is this threat?" he asked, keeping his voice hushed. Besonlor looked to her King and he could see the fear in her eyes.

"The granddaughter of the son of Palakrine has been discovered and she intends to attack the Realm," she whispered. The King and Queen looked to each other. "And the one the Overseer is training, is in charge of the Realms defense." The King took the Queens arm.

"Come to my office," he told Besonlor, and led the two woman to his office, which was just off from the large room they were in. The room that used to be Maltakrine's throne room.

———ᗯᗯᗺᗼᗻᗼᗺᗯᗯ———

Somora stood, leaning against the corner of the hut. He smiled as he looked to the balcony and saw Castope and Prateope walk out to the railing. His thoughts were on the words he had heard from Mestilia, his strongest talker, and Gapilarian, his best seer. They had both told him that the trainee of the Overseer was beginning his planning's, as what to do about the Dark City, and Castope. "Soon Castope," he whispered to himself; "you will learn the same as your father, grandfather and great grandfather. That the ways of Dark Magic are best used, when used quietly and secretly!" His smile grew as he turned from the two on the balcony and returned to his hut and continued his own planning's.

———ᗯᗯᗺᗼᗻᗼᗺᗯᗯ———

Castope held Prateope's hand as she led the girl out onto the balcony. When they reached the railing, Castope released the girls hand and placed both of hers on the top of the railing. "The day is coming Prateope, when we will rule the Realm and all of the Domains!" The sound that came from the girl should have been a chuckle, but it came out low in tone, and deadly. Prateope looked up to her mother and felt her own desires for what was to become of the Realm, Domains, and her mother! But, first she will support her mother's efforts to take the Realm, and then plan her own takings!

Pelkraen entered the Overseers office, it was midmorning. "What is it?" Mike asked the Meleret.

"Jastile asks to speak with you Overseer. She waits outside," Pelkraen told him. Mike nodded as Palysee stood.

"I must return to Drandysee's training; I must return to Drandysee's training," the Elder sang. Mike smiled to his old friend.

"I will walk you out," he said and the two left the palace, but Mike looked to the closed door of the reading room as they passed it. Palysee gave a bow to Jastile as he passed her and went out the gate. Mike stopped in front of the mate of Cartile. "What can I do for you Jastile?" he asked her. He saw the look of worry in her eyes as she lowered to be at a level where the Overseer didn't have to look up.

"I worry for Cartile," she told him. Mike felt her worries.

"What causes this worry Jastile?" he asked, the true concern for his friend shown in his question. Jastile looked to the ground for a moment and then lifted her eyes to his.

"What he was forced to do, with Chartile, hurts him, and he has trouble finding peace," she told him. Mike could hear her own pain for the death of her son. Mike nodded.

"Do you feel I should talk with him?" Mike asked. Jastile nodded.

"He respects you Overseer. Perhaps he can find peace if you help him find the way," she told him. Mike smiled at her.

"I will be honored to help my friend," he told her. "Return to him and I will come in a few minutes. I think between us, we will help him find the peace he needs." Jastile smiled, with a single nod and stood.

"Thank you Overseer," she said and leapt into the air. Mike watched as she flew to hers and Cartile's cave. He gave her time to reach the cave and then spelled himself to the opening to the cave. It would be late afternoon when he would leave, and he was pleased that his friend seemed better, when he did. When he returned to the palace, he was disappointed that the representatives had already left, but Heathers call to him, took his attentions from that disappointment.

———

Mike sat down at his desk and looked around, half hoping that Namson had left some evidence of the planning's of the group. Heather suddenly appeared in the office. "Daddy," she started; "Belthume is aware of the situation and Besonlor, their strongest talker, has told me that King Martoran would like to speak with you about what is being planned." Mike couldn't stop the chuckle that came.

"To tell the truth honey, I'm not real sure what is being planned," he said and Heather almost smiled, but the worry in her eyes restricted her efforts.

"Isn't Namson including you in his planning?" she asked cautiously. Mike smiled at her worry.

"You have to understand honey," Mike told her. "When I told Namson that he was to command what is done with the Dark City, I told him that it would be his decisions that would be followed." Heather sat in one of the chairs in front of the desk.

"Are you saying that Namson is now the Overseer?" she asked quietly, and Mike could hear the fear in her voice. He shook his head and smiled at her.

"No honey, I am still the Overseer. I have just allowed Namson to find his own answers. I know that when he has some sort of a solid plan, he will come to me and we will talk about it. If I agree, then that plan will be implemented." Mike's voice was calm and he saw Heather relax, slightly.

"So, what do I tell Besonlor?" she asked.

"Tell her to pass on to Martoran, that I would be very happy to meet with him. I have not been able to talk with anyone from Belthume since his parent's passing.

Perhaps, he may have an idea that Namson can use. Tell her to inform the King that Namson and I," Mike saw an instant desire in his daughters eyes; "and you, will come tomorrow, after the sun is high." Heather nodded, a small twinkle in her eye and she passed on his words.

———

After the others' had returned to their Domains, Namson and Glornina sat on the couch, reviewing everything that had been discussed. When they had a better idea of what was to be done, Namson called a faxlie messenger to him. Hastilear, a young faxlie that was larger than most and could fly faster than any other, came to him in the reading room. "Yes Namson, what can I do for you?' he asked, landing on the short table in front of the couch.

"I would ask that you travel to the elves, dragons, Natharian's, ogres, trolls, eagles, imps, and of course the fairy folk, telling the leaders of each, to meet with me here, on the rear terrace, just after sunrise," Namson told him. Hastilear nodded, with a small grin.

"I will do as you ask Namson," the faxlie stated. He bowed to Glornina and flew out of the window. Glornina took Namson's hand and he turned to her. He saw the concern in her eyes.

"Do not fear my love," he told her softly. She tried to smile but her worries wouldn't let her.

"What will come of this Namson?" she asked in a whisper. His arm came around her shoulder and he pulled her gently to him.

"Whatever will come my dear. We must be ready for anything that might be, and that includes staying strong for each other and those of the magical Domains." She looked into his eyes and found her smile.

"I swear to you, I will be strong," she whispered. He smiled with his nod and gently kissed her. There came a knock on the door. It opened and Mike and Heather entered.

———

Castope walked out on her balcony, just as the sun was setting. She took a deep breath and looked out over her city. Lights were coming from windows as her people began the cooking of their suppers. She smiled, sure that her plans were progressing just as she wanted.

CHAPTER FIVE

The representatives of the Domains, and their wives, were the first to arrive. The other races quickly followed. Namson stood and silence came to the meeting. He spoke to the races who had gathered, first. "As you are all aware, the daughter of the son of Saltakrine, Castope, is planning to attack the Realm, and all of the Domains," he said rather loudly. There were nodded heads and exchanged looks, throughout the group. "We," Namson waved his hand at the representatives; "are trying to work out a plan of defense. A defense that will be an aggression!" A small explosion of voices followed his statement. Namson raised his hands and again, silence came. "This Castope has more power in Dark Magic, than any of her ancestors and we cannot wait for her to make the first move. We must stop her before she can finalize her plans and attack us!" There were silent looks shared by all. "I will start by saying that if you are ever discussing our plans with any of your race and there is someone you do not know nearby, don't talk of the plans." All looked surprised. "We cannot take the chance that Castope has sent spies, trying to learn what we are about." Heads nodded. "We have started to map out the Dark City, by sending Pentilian and Pelinoria, to explore and examine the layout and defenses of the city, as well as the design of whatever palace, fortress or castle, Castope is using as her head quarters." All eyes looked to the two women, as they stood with the calling of their names.

"How can they do that?" Balsarlan asked in the hiss like voice of the Natharian's. Namson smiled at the very large creature. They all, human and races, remembered that when the battle with the Dark Forces of Palakrine had ended and Balsarlan and others' had come to Mike and asked for the right to stay among the new friends they had made in the Realm. How there had been some that worried about the great size of the creatures, but Mike had told all that the Natharian's offered much to the Realm and should be welcomed. They had been given an area north east of the city, in the large forest that was there, and the first thing they had done, after building their webs, was to build a large bridge over the Realm River. With the efforts of those who knew how to remove the stickiness of the webbing, the bridge changed the travel time to and from a large farming and artistic town to the northeast, from over a week, to just a day. They had been truly welcomed after that.

"Because they both have inherited their grandfather Zachia's ability of invisibility, that cannot be sensed," Namson told the leader of the Natharian tribe, in the Realm. "They can easily move through the city and then report back what they have seen as well as draw out maps." Namson turned to the two and nodded. They quickly gave their husbands a kiss and then disappeared. Even as accustom to the disappearances of those of magical powers, there were still a few that twitched at the sudden disappearance of the two. For the next several hours, Namson, Glornina, and the other representatives explained the beginnings of their plans. There were many of the races that added their thoughts to those plans. When the meeting broke, it was nearing midday. As they left the meeting, there were many conversations going on between the races.

As Castope, followed by Prateope, Rilatance, Castope's private talker, and then Ralsanac, entered the room, she looked over those who had gathered. The three Dremlorian generals, who would lead each of the three armies that would invade the Realm, their lieutenants, aides and talkers, were sitting to the three other sides of the large square table. They stood and bowed when Castope reached her chair. A male servant held her chair as she sat. Once she was seated, the rest sat down and all eyes were on her. None saw the two visitors, who had not been invited and were hiding in the room. Ralsanac passed a folder to her and she slowly opened it as she again let her eyes travel over all. She smiled as she looked to the contents of the folder. "General Braston," Castope started; "status of your preparations?"

"Army number one is on schedule and we are ready Mistress," the general to Castope's right said, trying to make his voice sound more resonant.

"Gurlin?' Castope asked the general across from her.

"Army number two is on schedule Mistress," the General replied, not having to try to make his voice resonant. It was deep and full of power. Castope nodded, without looking from the folder.

"Jepinran?" she asked the general to her left.

"Army number three is on schedule Mistress," the General said, not even bothering to hide his merely average voice.

"Good," Castope said as she meshed her fingers and placed her forearms on the folder. "I have decided that rather than have all of the Fire dragons, you each will have with your troops, be the leading forces through the portals, you will have them split into three waves." The Generals looked to each other first, in confusion, and then to Castope. "You will divide the dragons into three equal numbers. The first wave to be followed by a large number of troops. Then the second wave of dragons will pass through, giving support to the troops ahead of them, and they will be followed by an equaled sized number of troops as the first. The third wave of dragons will then pass through, giving support to the troops ahead of them, and they will be followed by a smaller number of troops. The last wave of troops should be a cleanup force, for most of the damage suffered by those of the Realm, should have already been done!" There were some of the aides that still looked confused, but all three Generals looked to Castope and joined in her smile.

Namson had already finished his lunch when Mike wiped his mouth and then placed his napkin next to his plate. As he reached for his tea cup, he looked to Namson and Glornina and smiled. "Are you ready for our journey to Belthume?" he asked Namson. Namson smiled and nodded, as did Glornina.

"I am looking forward to seeing where you began the battles against the Dark Magic," Glornina said softly to her great grandfather. Mike's smile showed some pain, for his memories.

"It was needed thing, but there were many hurt and killed in those battles," Mike told her. She dropped her eyes and then looked Namson, who had placed his hand on hers. She looked to Mike.

"I know grandpa, but it was the true beginning of Rightful Magic, and I would like to see where it began," she told him. Mike nodded as his smile returned to his face.

"Well, it looks as though you will," he said and stood. The rest followed his actions. He led them from the dining room, to his office. Mike went and sat behind the desk and Namson and Glornina took the two chairs in front of the desk. "As soon as Heather gets here, we'll go," Mike said to them. "So while we wait, is there anything you can tell of your plans?" He was looking to Namson when he asked. Namson smiled, slightly.

"We really haven't gotten too far in those yet and, if you don't mind, I would rather wait until we have something more definite to tell, before I do," Namson told him. Mike looked to his trainee for several seconds before he nodded his head. Heather's arrival saved Namson from further questioning.

"I've already told Besonlor that we would be coming soon," she announced to all. Mike grinned and stood. He led them out of the palace, to the grass just off from the terrace. He opened a portal there and they all passed through, to Belthume, just outside of the castle gates, where King Martoran, Queen Restone, Besonlor and two other people, a man and a woman, awaited them.

"Lord Overseer," Martoran said as he came to them, his hand extended; "it is so good to see you again." Mike gripped the hand of the man and thought of the last time he had seen him. The now man, was just fifteen when Mike and Gloreana had come to the funeral of Martoran's parents. Mike smiled and indicated the other three with him.

"My daughter Heather," he said, and those of Belthume bowed. Heather returned the bow, smiling at Besonlor. "The one I train to be Overseer, Namson and his wife Glornina, my great granddaughter." Mike indicated them and bows were exchanged. When straightened, all could see Martoran's eyes were quite wide as he looked to Glornina.

"You look very much like your great grandmother," he said, and all nodded. Martoran turned to Mike. "We were all saddened when word of her passing came to us. We offer our sincerest condolences." Mike bowed, with only his head, as his back wasn't going to allow any more than that. His emotions held his words as he fought back his tears. "Please, allow me to present my Queen, Restone," Martoran said, taking her arm. Bows were again exchanged. "Our strongest talker Besonlor." Bows were made. He pointed to the other two. "Our Black Dragon Rider Commander, Delakas and the General of our armies, Ransidar. Again bows were made.

"Please, come inside," Queen Restone said. "There are refreshments waiting." Those of the Realm smiled and nodded. Mike walked with the King and Queen. Heather had taken Besonlor's arm and they walked together, talking silently. Namson, Delakas and Ransidar, brought up the rear. As they passed through the gate, Mike could not stop himself from looking to the tower where he and his brother, sisters and cousin, had battle the monster Maltakrine, The tower where he had met the woman who would hold his heart from that time on. He felt a sadness and a loneliness, not having them with him now. They went on into the castle and to a rather small room that had two couches, facing each other, with a low table that was as long as the couches between them. Around the walls of the room were many varied and beautiful tapestries. There were several tables set with several different kinds of drink and snacks and there were at least a dozen servants standing by them.

"Please, have a seat," Martoran said. Mike and the others' sat on one couch and the King and the other's sat on the opposing one. The servants started to load trays when Mike held up his hand.

"I can't speak for the others," but we recently finished our mid day meal and I don't think I could eat another thing, but I wouldn't say no to a brandy," he told their hosts. Restone smiled and signaled the servants for a brandy.

"What about the rest of you, what can we get for you?" she asked. Heather said she could use a small brandy herself, and Namson and Glornina said that anything cold and wet would be appreciated. The King, Queen, talker and Black Dragon Commander, had a brandy each, but General Ransidar, a rather large individual, got up and stacked a plateful and returned to the couch. After all had their drinks, Martoran turned serious.

"We have heard of the threat to the Realm and the Domains," he said, looking to Mike. "Whatever you are planning, be it known that anything that Belthume can do to help, will be done." Mike chuckled and Namson and Glornina exchanged grins. Heather just looked to her father and then shrugged. Those of Belthume looked to Mike in confusion.

"I am honored by your offer," Mike told the King; "but Namson is planning the defense against Castope. You should talk with him." All of Belthume looked to the young Namson and then back to Mike.

"Is he the new Overseer?" Martoran asked, almost whispering. It was Namson's turn to chuckle. Glornina and Heather joined in, quietly.

"Not yet," Namson said. "The overseer has placed his trust in me and he will review my final plan before any action is taken. It is a great honor he gives me and I do not intend to let him down!" Mike actually blushed. "We have not had the time to get much more than a basic idea of what we want to accomplish yet, but I can tell you this, we are going after her, not waiting for her to pick the time best for her," Namson told them. Martoran's brows were higher than they were a minute ago. He glanced to Mike, who was taking a sip of brandy. He returned his eyes to Namson.

"What can we do to help?" he asked calmly, but all could see that he really wasn't all that calm. Namson looked to him and a small grin came to his lips.

I'm not real sure yet, but if you would like, you could send a representative to our meetings. That way you could aide with ideas and we all would have a better idea of what your Domain could do," Namson told the king. Martoran leaned forward and looked to his General, who had been steadily eating during the conversation, and paying close attention to what was being said. Even before Martoran asked, the General spoke.

"I know the perfect one to send to these meetings, Your Highness," he said quietly, looking steadily at Namson. He turned to his King. "Kailen, my first lieutenant and a very smart officer!" Ransidar said.

"If he is married, please have him bring his wife as well," Glornina said. The General bowed and then took another bite from the sandwich he was holding.

"There will be another meeting this afternoon, if you will send him then, we can start to include him in the planning's," Namson told the General. Ransidar quickly finished chewing and turned to Martoran.

"If you will excuse me, Your Highness, I will go and inform Kailen to prepare." The King nodded and the General stood, taking several sandwiches with him. He bowed to those of the Realm and left the room. The lieutenant and the general returned before Mike and the others' had left. The lieutenant brought a very lovely young woman, who looked as though she was fifteen years old. The lieutenant didn't look much older than that himself.

"Your Majesty," Delakas said, standing. "With your permission, I would like to attend these meetings as well. I have heard of the wisdom and power of the Realm dragons and would like a chance to see this myself, as well as allowing the Black Dragon leader, and my friend, Bursanlac a chance to meet with the dragon leader there." Martoran looked to Mike and then Namson. Namson looked to the Overseer and Mike nodded.

"I believe that yours and Bursanlac's input can be nothing but an advantage to all," Namson told the woman and looked to the King. "I would welcome the Black Dragon Riders leader in our meetings," he told Martoran. The King smiled with his nod and looked to Delakas.

"Prepare your dragon," he told her. "When you are ready, I shall open a portal for you." She smiled, bowed and left the room. "We now have close to a hundred of the Black

Dragons, and their riders," the King told Namson, with a smile of pride. All those of the Realm lifted their brows at that news.

"We could use the extra dragons," Glornina whispered to Namson, as her hand closed on his arm. He glanced at her with a nod and a grin.

"Also," the King continued; "Ransidar is a excellent strategist and the lieutenant Kailen he mentioned, is as good!" Namson and Mike exchanged quick looks and both smiled as Glornina's hands closed tighter on Namson's arm. "I am sure that the armies of Belthume will also be a benefit to your campaign." Namson bowed to the King. It was about an hour later, when those of the Realm returned to the Realm, after Mike had taken Namson and Glornina to the tower where the battle with Maltakrine had occurred.

Namson and Glornina dragged the wide eyed lieutenant and his young bride to the rear terrace, where the meeting was already in progress. The lieutenant and wife were a little nervous when they saw the Natharian's, but with an explanation, settled quickly. Though they did jump, a little, when Pentilian and Pelinoria appeared and started to draw maps of what they had seen that day. Namson and Glornina were very surprised when Kailen, and his wife, Mistilane, quickly adapted to the situation and started giving ideas, that turned out to be quite useful.

CHAPTER SIX

Time passed. For many, it seemed to drag by, but for Namson, it was traveling at a speed that could not be imagine. As Pentilian and Pelinoria brought more and more information about the Dark City, Namson's plans became clearer. He was continually updating the races he had selected to be part of the operation. He was constantly in a meeting with one, or more, from the different Domains. Merlintile, Bursanlac, and Dartile, of the Plain, were also having their meetings, as more of their role in the coming battle was explained to them. All of the races were coordinating their plans, to increase their effectiveness in the assault on the Dark City. Glornina stayed by Namson's side as much as she could, but there were times that she too had specific things that needed to be done.

It had been close to a year, a year of planning and plotting of those of Rightful Magic, led by Namson, when Namson finally called for a meeting with Mike. "I mean no disrespect Mike," Namson started, after they had sat; "but I think it best that you stay and act as leader for a defense, in case the Dark Forces manage a strike against the Realm," Namson said softly, as they sat in the office that used to be Mike's. The Overseer had been expecting this and to be honest, was relieved. He nodded. He had been catching bits and pieces of Namson's plans, but not all of them, and he was satisfied with what little he had heard so far.

"The fighting of wars must be done by the young," he said softly, a small smile on his lips.

"I don't mean that you are not . . . ." Mike held up his hand to the young Overseer.

"There is no need to apologize Namson," Mike told him. "I am having enough troubles getting around the palace, I don't even want to think about running around a battle field." The smile stayed on his face. "When do you plan your attack?" he asked Namson. Namson looked to the man who held his greatest respect.

"In three days, at dawn," he said simply. Mike lifted his brows.

"So soon?" he asked. "Are you that prepared already?" Namson nodded.

"We have managed to get into the Dark City and do considerable scouting of the city and Castope's fortress." Mike's brows went up again as he sat up straighter.

"When did you do that, and who?" he asked with an awed voice, knowing they had not had use of the Seeing Stone. Namson smiled softly.

"Pentilian and Pelinoria have both inherited their grandfather Zachia's talent of invisibility," Namson said quietly. Mike nodded as the death of his son returned painfully to his heart. He cleared his throat.

"Then you have figured out your attack pattern?" he asked, his voice riddled with his emotions. Namson nodded.

"The first thing you need to know is that not all of the those of the Dark City are with Castope. This includes Cartope, the oldest daughter of Castope, and Morsalon." Namson nodded to Mike at the naming of the son of Charlesia and Mensalon. "There seems to be another group, and what their purpose is, I do not know, for neither Pentilian nor Pelinoria could learn anything about them.

The city is backed by a very large lake and it is one of the only two ways out of the city, as there are steep mountains to the north and south of the city," Namson stated, pulling a map from the drawer of the desk and laying it out so Mike could see it. "We will open two portals each, to the north and south sides of the valley, and two out passed the Fire Dragons caves, which is the other way out of the city. There will also be one opened at the rear of the fortress and with the map we have made from Pentilian and Penoria's spying, invade the fortress directly. The strongest of magical powers will be in that group, to try and take Castope. The dragons will go first through the portals around the city, flaming, while those with the cutting lights will be second through the ones in front of the fire dragons caves, riding eagles. Vralar and the eagles are very eager to do this.!" Namson said and Mike nodded with a small grin, that held worry. "The Natharian's will be next from all portals. From the other four, to the north and south, the rest shall follow the Natharian's and we shall invade with the surprise of the cities sudden awakening and that should disrupt them enough that many will try to flee to the lake. There are fishing vessels there and I'm sure that they will try to escape with those. Those ships are the second targets for some of the dragons," Namson told him. "The dragons will burn the ships and then return and flame the city as they pass over, continuing the panic that is sure to be and then on to the caves to cover the cutters." Mike looked over the map and then raised his eyes to Namson. He stared into the young man's eyes for awhile and then nodded, as a pained smile formed on his face.

Castope looked from the balcony and smiled with a comfort that almost overwhelmed her. Her thoughts went to the joy she would have with the destruction of the Realm, the slaying of the young Overseer and all that would follow him. She had a very strong feeling that the old Overseer was near his death, and she was anxious to begin her attack. Ralsanac met with those he had awoken from the coma he had induced. They plotted to free Cartope and Morsalon, before Castope could mate the girl to any Demons. Somora called his followers and told them that they must prepare, for their time of escape was coming closer.

Cranedoran didn't want to get out of his bed. With his age, which was the same as the Overseers, he had finally found a position where things didn't hurt and he was happy. He had felt and heard Xanaloren rise earlier and he knew she attended to the beginning of the castle staffs day. Yes, he was quite happy where he was, until the sounds of clashing swords and yelling brought his eyes wide open. He groaned with his efforts as he left the bed and went to the open bedroom window. Looking out, he saw that there were at least five hundred people, both men and women, battling in the huge court yard below, and the grasses that surrounded the castle. He immediately thought the Dark forces had attacked in the night. Xanaloren's voice calmed him.

"Crendosa and Croldena exercise the army," she told him, coming through the door with a tray that held a cup and a hot beverage container on it. "They are teaching them to use something other than magic, so they could be prepared for anything," she added, setting the tray on the table near Cranedoran. The king looked back to the mayhem and could see that there were many that also practiced with the sheathed bladed staffs. He slowly shook his head and returned to the bed and sat down, as his wife and Queen, poured his coffee into the cup and then brought it to him. He smiled his thanks as he took the cup and took his first drink. "They attack in days my King," she told him as she sat down next to him. Cranedoran sprayed the mouthful of coffee across the room and looked to her wide eyed.

"What?" he tried to yell, but it came out as a squeak. She almost managed a smile as she looked to him and nodded.

"Crendosa told me this morning at breakfast," she said. "They have been planning for a year and they are ready to attack." She looked to her hands that worried a napkin she held. "The army is due to travel to the Realm in two days and our great grandson, Croldena is to be their commander. They will attack the Dark City the following morning, at sunrise." Her eyes began to fill with the tears of her worry. He put his arm around her shoulders. He didn't know what to say to her, so he just held her and listened to the sounds of war that came through the window.

<hr />

"Elamson, you will be needed here, to guide the people of Calisonnos, if the Dark City were to launch a counter attack against this Domain," Vandora told him and Gerpinos nodded her agreement. Ferlinos looked to her daughter with fear in heart. She did not like the idea that Gerpinos was going with Vandora, on the attack of the Dark City.

"Mama, don't you see the wisdom of Vandora's decision?" Gerpinos asked her mother. Ferlinos fought her fear and nodded first to her and then to Elamson.

"They are right my husband. Vandora must lead our army on the attack," she told Elamson. He looked to her and she saw the same fear in his eyes that she felt in her heart.

"Tell me again the plan that you young have devised," Elamson said, turning back to Vandora. The younger man nodded.

"The armies of Calisonnos will be going to Vistalin. There, the armies of Calisonnos and the combined armies of all the Domains of Vistalin will travel through the two portals to the south side of the Dark City. The armies of Dolaris and Ventoria will come through the two portals to the north of the Dark City. The armies of Corsendora and the Realm and Belthume, will come through the two portals that front the fire dragons caves, east of the city. This attack will include an army of Elves, trolls and others with cutting weapons. An army of dragons from the Realm, Plain and Belthume, will pass through the portals north and south of the city first and cause all kinds of havoc with their flaming. There will be a band of twelve, consisting of those with the most powerful of Magical talents, led by Namson and Glornina, who will come through a portal behind the fortress and enter it, going after Castope directly." Vandora looked to Elamson and smiled. "It is a good plan, but all the Domains of rightful magic must be able to handle any counter attack that might come from the Dark Forces." Elamson nodded his agreement and looked to Gerpinos.

"Do you have to go? Why can't you stay here, with us?" Ferlinos didn't even look to her daughter, for she knew what her answer was to be.

"He is my husband and where he must fight, I must fight by his side," Gerpinos told her father, her head lifting with her truth. Elamson nodded and sat next to his wife.

"When do you leave?" he asked the floor.

"In two days," Vandora answered softly.

———

"You must be with your father." Tyrus told Heather softly. She looked to him and tears formed.

"My place is with you," she told him. Tyrus shook his head.

"Prestilon will lead our army to the Dark City. Sonilon and I will handle what defense there must be, here. You must be with your father, for you, and for him," he told her. "If you stay here, your heart and mind will be with him and you will be of no use to even yourself." She looked to him as tears rolled down her cheeks. He took her into his arms and she sobbed for her torn loyalties.

———

In the South West Domain of Vistalin, Brei and Crondasa watched as their grandson, Crandon, trained their army. Crondasa's arm held her. He suddenly felt her tremble. "What is it my love?" he asked, worry in his voice. She could not speak at first and when she did, her words were filtered through her tears.

"They are too young," she said simply. He tightened his arm on her shoulders.

"They are the age you were when you fought Palakrine," he told her gently. She nodded, ignoring her tears.

"That was too young," she whispered. He turned her and took her into his arms. His thoughts could only agree with her.

⸻

Sen had come to visit her younger brother, Matsar, and his wife, Drayson, in the South East Domain of Vistalin. The three now stood on the edge of the open pasture and watched as their grandson, Norson, trained with the armies of the South East domain. Matsar's arm circled Drayson's shoulders.

"They know what they are about," Sen said quietly. Matsar nodded as Drayson brought her hand to her mouth and lowered her eyes to the ground. "I have seen the same dedication from Morgan and Natoria's grandson, Tarson, as he trains the army of the Realm and Belthume." Her words cracked with her fears. Matsar tightened his arm around Drayson as her crying was heard and Sen took and held tightly to Matsar's other arm. He nodded his understanding, for his words would not come from his fearful mind.

⸻

Quoslon and Xanalenor stood on the front terrace of the castle and watched as their son, Edward put the army of the North West Domain through its training. "Oh Quoslon, what is to become of our son?" Xanalenor asked in a whisper. He put his arm around her.

"What has become of us all," he told her. She looked to him, fearing what she saw in his eyes.

"Quoslon?" she asked, still in a worried whisper. He looked to her, his eyes softening and he tried to smile.

"He will do what has been done before, but this time, there is a chance to finally be rid of the Dark Magic, completely." His voice was soft but intense. "All that are known to hold power in the Dark Magic are in the Dark City." The tears slowly came from her eyes as she nodded and looked back to her son.

"He's so young," she whispered and he nodded, trying brace himself against his own fears for their son.

—⁂—

Mike, Palysee and Drandysee watched the training of the Realms armies. Farther away, nearer the eastern mountains, they could see the dragons practicing their moves. Mike and Palysee both sat in chairs, in the shade.

"Namson has instructed them well; Namson has instructed them well." Drandysee sang with assurance. Both Mike and Palysee nodded their agreement, without looking to the newly promoted Elder.

"When we fought, I did not feel fear; when we fought, I did not feel fear," Palysee sang softly. Mike smiled and looked to his old friend.

"I did," he told the Wingless who had called him to the Realm. Palysee returned his look and smiled as well.

"I should tell you; I should tell you," Palysee sang, turning back to the skirmishes before them. "That when you first came, I doubted your success; that when you first came, I doubted your success." Mike turned to him with a half smile and lifted brows.

"Really?" he asked and Palysee nodded. His grin grew as he looked back at Mike.

"When you all started to pour out of that portal; when you all started to pour out of that portal. I worried about the young faces I saw; I worried about the young faces I saw." Mike chuckled and nodded.

"You hid your concerns well my friend," Mike told him and Palysee chuckled

"It was your facing with the large sheep that convinced me that the Overseer had come; it was your facing with the large sheep that convinced me that the Overseer had come," Palysee sang quietly. Mike again looked to the Wingless with surprise. Palysee nodded. "I could see your anger and yet you kept control; I could see your anger and yet you kept control." Mike smiled as he thought of that event.

"Daddy," Heather reprimanded, suddenly appearing to Mike's right and causing both her father and Palysee to jump. She had been looking for him for quite a while, before someone finally told her where he was. "What are you doing out here? You could catch a chill." Mike sighed as Drandysee and Palysee chuckled. "And you too Palysee," she added. "Don't you two think about what you do?" Palysee turned to Heather with a glare as Drandysee chuckled louder and Mike joined him. "Come on, I'm taking you back to the palace," Heather said as she took Mike's arm. Mike pulled his arm from her.

"I *am*, the Overseer and I am still quite capable of taking care of myself young lady," Mike told Heather and she smirked.

"Really?" she asked crossing her arms over her chest. "You're not even sitting in the sun to stay warm, either of you."

"I would be sweating like a virgin in a cage full of Demons," Mike told her, glaring and beginning to lose his temper. Heather dropped her arms and looked to her father.

"I'm just worried about you daddy," she told him, dropping her eyes. Mike lost his building anger and sighed.

"You might as well admit defeat; you might as well admit defeat," Palysee sang in a whisper and Mike grinned and nodded.

"Alright honey, I'll go with you, but I'm not an invalid, yet," he told her and she nodded and helped him from the chair.

"Whatever you say daddy," she whispered and winked at Drandysee, who covered his laughter with amazing skill. "Besides, Namson wants to speak with you," she threw in and they disappeared. Drandysee wrestled a complaining Palysee from his chair and led him to the Elders building. The following morning, the armies of Corsendora arrived in the Realm, the armies of Calisonnos arrived on Vistalin and the armies of Dolaris arrived in Ventoria. The dragons of the Realm, Plain and Belthume, with their riders, divided their numbers, near to two hundred, and those who needed, were sent to Vistalin and Ventoria. There were many Natharian's from their home Domain as well as from each of the Domains they had been welcomed, and they too were divided between the three Domains, where the assaults were to be launched. The elves, eagles, wolves', trolls, imps and fairy folk were also divided and sent to the proper Domains.

⁂

The waking of the armies in the Realm, Vistalin and Ventoria began several hours before the sun was to rise. There were a few groggy heads from lack of sleep and some from too much brandy or other drinks, but they all got up willingly and ate a filling breakfast. Mike and Namson had met in the Overseers office the night before and Namson had again explained the attack, including those who were to go after Castope directly. Himself and Glornina, Dalynia, Taylor and Johnny, Meligan and

Micky, Pelinoria, Meladiana, Prelilian, Xanaporia and Pentilian. Pentilian would go first, invisibly, to notify all when the sun cleared the horizon of the Dark City. These were the twelve who possessed the strongest of magical talents. These were the twelve who would enter Castope's fortress and seek out Castope and any that may be the most dangerous. Mike looked the young man before him. He called his daughter to him.

"What is it daddy?" Heather asked as she appeared in the room.

"Pass on my words now," he told her and she nodded, looking from him to Namson, fearing what she was going to hear.

"From this moment on, Namson is now the declared Overseer of the Realm!" Mike stated and extended his hand to the new Overseer. Heather told all Domains the words her father had asked her to, but she had to fight the tears that came to her. She realized that her father had just given away the only reason he still had to live.

Carla, Edward's wife and Paul and Glory's daughter, was to act as the coordinating talker and that morning she was already at work talking with Ventoria and Vistalin, as well as Namson and the talkers with each of the armies. She wasn't as powerful as Heather, but she was pretty damn close. Heather, who had met with Carla the night before, prior to her father's announcement, giving her tips and getting her to include Heather in her talking, now stood with Mike in the entry hall of the palace. Namson and the other eleven came from the office and stopped in front of Mike. He looked to each of them, fighting his fear for what they faced.

"Every heart and mind goes with you all," he finally told those before him. They all nodded and tried to smile, but the reality of what they were about to do was bearing down on them.

"We know and feel all with us and welcome it, for it gives us strength," Namson told Mike. He quickly bowed to Heather and led the procession from the palace just as the sky was beginning to lighten. Mike and Heather followed them and stopped on the front terrace of the palace. They couldn't see the Realm and Belthume armies, for they were in the field near the Elders residence, but they could see the ghost like figures of the circling dragons. Mike and Heather watched the twelve as they prepared. Pentilian disappeared as the rest lined up, two abreast. Heather was sending her father all she heard from Carla and any others' she could pick up. "Carla, set the ready." Namson said both mentally and out loud.

"All are ready Namson," Carla told him. He looked to the sky. Watching the sun in the Realm and waiting for Pentilian's word the sun was breaking the horizon of the Dark City.

"Daddy, I'm scared," Heather whispered to Mike.

"So am I honey, so am I," he whispered back.

"Pentilian says now." Carla told Namson. He nodded

"On three," he told those with him and Carla, who relayed his command to all Domains. He lifted his hands and began his count. Mike saw the dragons begin their dive. "One, two, three." Namson cried out the three, and seven portals opened in three Domains and closed as quickly as all had passed through. The one Namson and the ten had entered was the first to close and Mike and Heather listened to the silence that closed in on them, as a tomb. They looked to each other and then Carla started coordinating messages and they were barraged with information from the Dark City.

Namson stepped from the portal, followed by the other ten. The portal closed as they all looked around in the darkness behind the Fortress, not three feet from the rear door. They all heard the locking bolt being pulled back and the door swung open and they saw the smiling face of Pentilian. She beckoned them in as the sounds of roaring and flaming dragons entering the city were heard. Once inside, they could barely hear the screams of the people as they woke to the flames. They followed the route they had all studied thoroughly. Quickly, the sounds of six charging armies told them all they needed to know

Morsalon had been working on opening the cell door every chance he was left unwatched. This night had been no different. Suddenly, a hand closed on the one he had extended outside the cell. He gasped quietly and tried to jerk his hand back. "Relax, it is me." Ralsanac whispered.

"Step back, I know the spell to open it," he added and Morsalon stepped back, glancing to the nearby window. He could see the sky just beginning to lighten and he knew Castope would wake with the suns appearance. The click of the lock opening sounded as an explosion to Morsalon's ears. Both he and Ralsanac froze and looked to Castope's bedroom door. Seconds seemed as hours as they stared at the door. Finally, Morsalon slowly pushed open the door and they crossed to Cartope's cell. Morsalon took the extended hand of the girl as Ralsanac worked his magic on the lock. Cartope no longer tried to cover her nakedness, for Castope had ordered her stripped as soon as she and Prateope had returned to her quarters. The guards hands had enjoyed more than just tearing the girls clothes from her as Prateope smiled at Cartope's cries caused by the guards handling.

"I've finished my first cycle. She will bring the Demons today. Please don't let her do this to me," she whispered her plea to him. The click of the lock opening was covered by the roaring of dragons entering the city. All three looked wide eyed to the bedroom door that had suddenly been thrown open. A naked Castope screamed and threw a blast spell at them. Cartope deflected the spell as Ralsanac yanked open the door. Grabbing Cartope, Morsalon and Ralsanac fled for the door out of Castope's quarters. Cartope spelled clothes to herself as she ran. Castope was so enraged, the second blast spell she sent, missed the three completely, blasting a hole in the wall, next to the door they passed through. They turned the other direction and ran as fast as they could. Castope turned back to the whimpering sounds of the guard she had bedded the night before. She vented her rage on him, not even concerned about the mess he made of the headboard. She spelled clothes to herself and chased after the fleeing trio, as the sounds of six armies charging into her city were heard.

———∼∙✧∙✧✦✧∙✧∙∽———

Young Prateope woke to the sounds of the dragons. Her heart raced, but her thoughts were calm. A small smile came to her lips as her thoughts were sent to the selected ones. She calmly dressed as the answering messages returned to her. She knew what was happening, for Deligarn, her young sensor had been tracking the actions of a few in the Realm. Her grin grew as she thought of the surprise her mother was about to receive, but she was sure that in the end, her mother would defeat the attacking forces. She casually headed for the designated meeting place as her smile grew wider. Her actions were not the only secretive gathering, though, the other had begun long before the attack had come.

———∼∙✧∙✧✦✧∙✧∙∽———

Heather sat up straight in the chair, her eyes opening wider than they should be. Mike looked to her.

"Tommy says that there is one, in the Dark City that plots an attack on the Realm," she whispered to her father.

"Does he know who?" Mike asked her calmly. Heather passed the question on. Seconds passed and then Heather nodded and looked to Mike.

"Castope's youngest daughter, Prateope," she said. Mike nodded.

"Let's get everybody ready then," he told her and Heather began to alert all she could, including the other Domains, asking for any one they could spare.

———————

The first of many Fire Dragons, stuck its head from the opening of the caves east of the Dark City, at the sound of the incoming dragons roars and flaming. Twenty beams reached out and severed the heads that were coming to fire. The fallen burning bodies had to be shoved by the ones behind and their heads fell as they began to exit, adding to the number of bodies that blocked the entrances. None of the attacking forces saw the three that snuck from a cave that was much closer to the city, or the four that had slipped away long before attacking forces had come and joined another group that was quite large in number, at the base of the southern mountains. The three quickly and without firing, traveled to the meeting place their young Mistress had planned.

———————

The incoming dragons flew about the city, flaming any building or group of people, Demons or Goblins they saw. They didn't see the many sorcerers and sorceresses, Dremlors and at least a dozen of both demons and goblins that had already snuck off. The large amulets the dragons wore, absorbed the blast spells thrown at them from the ground, plus many carried elves with reflectors, the dragons of Belthume carried their riders, also with reflectors, and they were very successful at sending the amplified spells back to the issuers. When the Natharian's and the armies, casting blast spells, swinging bladed staffs and swords came charging into the city, four of the dragons turned from the city and started for the harbor they could see from their height. There, they began to flame the boats that could offer escape for those of the city. When all were burning, they turned back, rejoining those who still flamed the city. They veered slightly and flamed the Fortress as they neared. A dragons call was issued and half of the dragons turned to the Fire Dragons caves.

—⁓⊹◦❈⊙◐❉◑⊙❈◦⊹⁓—

The Fire Dragons had managed to get some of their numbers from the caves and were trying to destroy the attacking forces by flame and talon. They were not succeeding very well when the attacking dragons arrived. Some of the Fire Dragons tried to surrender, but the Natharian's, the cutting beams and blast spells, denied them. Within a half an hour, all of the Fire Dragons were destroyed, except for the three who were joining up with their young Mistresses small army and the four that had joined with the other band that had gathered together. The attacking forces now turned to join the battle in the city, leaving behind a search group to verify that all of the Fire Dragons had indeed been destroyed. One cave at a time, they entered and searched thoroughly.

The six portals of the attacking forces had been placed so as to form a half circle that covered the north, east and south of the city evenly. The incoming quickly spread out, cutting off any possible escape between their ranks. The armies advanced quickly, but carefully. A second wave followed. They were to make sure that none had hidden, waiting for the first ones through the portals to pass. The wolves', imps and fairy folk, were very effective at finding those who had hidden. The soldiers with them captured many sorcerers and sorceresses and herded them to designated places and guarded them well. No Demon or Goblin was allowed to live. Imps played a major role in making sure of this, for they had a strong sense of both. One of hatred, the other, fear. The Dark Forces, so prepared to be an attacking force were not prepared to be a defending one. Add the fact that they had been awoken from a deep sleep by the attack, they were very disoriented and frightened. The battle of the Dark City was brutal, bloody, and very one sided.

<hr />

The hallways of the Fortress were quite wide and the twelve were able to travel three abreast. When they came to a cross hallway, Namson would send two in both directions, to make sure that there was no danger of someone coming in behind them. When the returning dragons began to flame the Fortress, which was completely made of wood, the hallways quickly filled with panicking guards, sorcerers, sorceresses and Dremlors. Namson, Glornina and Dalynia, who were the front row of three, cast blast spells forward as fast as they could. Johnny, Meladiana and Meligan, the three in the row behind, placed one of their hands on their shoulders, giving the front three the added support of their magical power. They also extended their other hand backwards and held the hands of Micky, Pelinoria and Pentilian, who were walking backwards with their other hands on the shoulders of Prelilian, Taylor and Xanaporia, who were also walking backwards and casting blast spells at any they saw behind them. Thus they advanced. The leading six guiding the trailing six.

———

"In here," Ralsanac yelled over the screams of panicking people in the halls. Ralsanac held one of Cartope's hands and pulled her up short as he pushed open what looked like a section of wall. Morsalon, who had only just barely heard Ralsanac's yell, couldn't stop that quick and as he held Cartope's other hand, stretched Cartope to the point where their hands separated. Cartope caught the door before it could close and looked to him.

"Come on," she yelled at him. He looked to her and then back down the hall they had just come through. The screaming threats of Castope came clearly over the panicked shrieks of the others'. He looked back to her and he smiled as he pushed her hand from the door.

"Ralsanac, get her away!" he yelled and let the door close. He turned to the sounds of the advancing Castope. The last that Cartope saw of her father was the determined look on his face as he faced the coming Castope. Ralsanac pulled her to the ladder that went down through the floor and he pulled her down after him. She followed with tears trying to steal her vision.

"Tommy," Heather called to him with thought and voice. "Can you tell where she will open the portal?" There was a hesitation. "Tommy, can you hear me?" she asked again, trying to keep her thoughts calm.

"There's too much going on." Tommy told her. "There are too many with the ability to talk and they are panicking. I can't read through them," his voice held the edge of panic. Heather glanced to her father who was watching her calmly.

"Tommy can't read through the panicked voices of the city," she told him. Mike smiled slightly and nodded.

"Morsalon must have given them all a complete description of Realm City and the area around it. I think this girl is smart enough to know that if she entered the city directly, there would be too many to deal with. I think she will open her portal outside the city, gather her forces carefully and plan after she is here," Mike told her as he thought. "Now where could Morsalon have told them, that would give this girl the place and time she would need to plan?" he asked himself as well as the others' who were stuffed into his office.

"The small forest that sits center of the plain, not far from the Elders building; the small forest that sits center of the plain, not far from the Elders building!" Drandysee stated, looking to Mike. Mike nodded and smiled at him.

"That's definitely a good place for her to come and Morsalon would have known it well," Mike said. He turned to Heather. "Pass on to our forces that they are to find a place of hiding, to watch that forest," he told her and she sent the order to all that now prepared to fight this assault. Those in the office who could, spelled themselves there. The others' ran, rode or flew.

Prateope smiled as she looked over the gathered. "When we arrive, you all must get into the trees as quickly as possible. We will plan better once we have looked at all that would resist us." Her smile widened. "There will a surprise waiting for those who would assault my mother, when they flee, back to the Realm." There was an agreeing guttural laughter from them all, as Prateope opened the portal and the small army passed into the Realm.

Somora looked over the ones gathered in front opening of the hidden tunnel, at the base of the southern mountains and smiled. Those in front of him, smiled with him. "We will find our own way and we are not to be fooled by the stupidity of those who attack straight on," he told them, having to yell for all to hear over the sounds of battle. "We will win by gently finding our way among those who rule and when the time is right, we will take control!" Perilia looked to her chosen, holding Dospora's hand and she too looked to their shared mate. They quickly exchanged a look and swelled with their pride of the new King, as they and the sixty Dremlors, sorcerers, sorceresses, twelve each of Goblins and Demons, plus four fire dragons, followed their King into the tunnel.

Tarson and Croldena met near the burning Fortress, nearly two hours after the assault had begun. Edward, Crandon, Prestilon, Norson, Jarsalon and Vandora, with Gerpinos beside him, joined them in a few minutes. The sounds of their armies chasing down the last of the resistance came to them as they looked at the burning building. Vandora broke the silence of the group.

"Do you think they got her and got out?" he asked any who chose to answer.

"There's been no word from Carla and I've been asking," Edward said and all heard the worry in his words. "All she says is that they have not talked to her recently."

"Well, I think they succeeded," Jarsalon stated. "Or we would have heard something."

"I hope you're right," Tarson said softly. "I don't like the idea of losing an Overseer the day after we get him." The others looked to him, trying to figure out if he was trying to be funny.

"What's everybody looking at?" Namson asked as he and the other eleven walked to the group from the south.

"Haven't you never seen a burning building before?" The ten looked to them wide eyed and then gave a very loud cheer as they looked into the eyes of the twelve. Hugs were quickly shared by all. After the hugs, they all turned back to the remnants of the burning Fortress.

"Did you get her?" Tarson asked.

"Namson got her," Micky said. "The rest of us were kinda busy with all the rest." Tarson and the other commanders looked to their new Overseer. Namson almost made the smile he was sure he didn't want.

"Not now, later," he told them as he looked into Glornina's eyes. She smiled and nodded as she came into his arms.

～～✦～✦～✦～～

Prateope's army quickly moved into the forest, as the portal had been opened just feet from the edge of it. There were many eyes watching as they did. Prateope looked around the area and saw nothing that seemed a threat.

"Prentastar, you look the closest to the dragons here," she said to the closest Fire Dragon. "Slip out behind the trees and fly east first, then circle back over the city and see what's happening there." The dragon in question nodded and went back the way he had come. Once clear of the trees, he leapt into the air and headed east. Prateope and the others watched his flight and smiled. They really should have been looking the other way. If they had been, they would have seen Cartile take flight from behind the Elders building. Quickly getting much higher than Prentastar, he kept watch on the dragon from the Dark City. Mike and Heather watched the dragon as it started east and slowly banked and started to fly over Realm City.

"Tell everyone to stay out of sight until that dragon returns," Mike told his daughter. She nodded and passed on his order. There were a few who looked to him questioningly. He smiled. "When he returns, he will tell Prateope that all is quiet and the city is wide open to be taken. She will of course, enjoy that news and begin to set her forces to a plan to take the city, not expecting any resistance." There were many nods, including Heathers. "When they clear the trees, then we will attack!" Mike's voice took a very intense edge. Heather looked to her father with concern.

Prentastar stayed high, so as to make it more difficult for anyone to see his difference from the Realm dragons. His sharp dragons sight made it easy for him to see that the city seemed quiet. There seemed no preparations for defense being made. He smiled as he banked again and headed back east and dropping down. He landed behind the forest and went to Prateope. None had seen the very high, circling Cartile.

"They make no preparations at all. They move about as any other day," he told her with a grin. She returned his grin and turned to her army.

"We will leave these trees and enter the city as though we belong there. Once in the city we will attack with a viciousness that will be seared into the memories of any who survive and I don't want many of them," she hissed at her troops and they grinned with their desire to kill. She pointed to a couple of Dremlors, that they should lead the parade into the city. She planned to stay to the center of the group. The designated two stepped from the trees and strode towards the city, the rest followed them.

"Ready all," Mike commanded and Heather alerted all of their forces. When the dragons cleared the trees Mike braced himself. "Now," he said and started out of hiding. Heather told the rest and the defending troops charged from their places of concealment, throwing blast spells and anything else they could get their hands on. There was a moment of surprise from Prateope's forces, but they quickly recovered and returned spells. The elves, who held reflectors, had taken the front of Realms defenses and the Dark forces spells were sent back to them, many times the power they had originally held. Heather stayed near her father as they both hurled their spells at the invaders and closed the distance. As they neared, Mike saw a Dremlor rise from the ground and cast a blast spell at Heather. He lunged in front of her and Heather was driven to the ground by the impact of the lifeless body of her father. When they had landed, Heather found her arms and hands pinned under her father. She cried out as she looked to the closed eyes of Mike.

"The great Overseer has been destroyed by the power of the Dark Magic!" Prateope cried out as she neared. Heather turned her tear filled eyes to her.

"There is no victory for you here!" she screamed at the evil twisted sneer of Prateope. "For the new Overseer now destroys your witch mother and all the evil she tried to bring to life. You are the one beaten by the Dark Magic, for you cannot defeat the Rightful Magic!" Prateope twitched only slightly at Heathers words. Her evil sneer returned as she lifted her hands to Heather.

"I am not defeated!" Prateope screamed and sent her blast spell, killing Heather. She threw her head back to scream her victory and looked up at the rapidly descending four sets of talons. Her eyes saw them, but her mind did not understand. She didn't even have time to scream as Nalatile's talons closed around her body and tore it into four evenly sized pieces. It did not take long for the rest of the Dark forces to be beaten once the death of Prateope had been seen. The Fire Dragons could not fight against the beams that cut them into pieces, except for Prentastar. He tried to fly away, but Cartile swooped down and caught him and killed the smaller, terrified Fire Dragon, tearing him apart in the air.

Those who had survived the battle, gathered around the bodies of Mike and Heather. Tears fell as the word of the deaths was passed to all of the Domains. A portal opened and Tyrus rushed from it. He dropped to his knees beside his wife and wept. No one moved for a long time. They couldn't for their sobbing. Drandysee was the only one who felt Palysee's death, for the once Elder was unable to stand the loss of his very close friend.

"Mike and Heather have been killed!" Carla's words screamed into all their minds. They all looked to each other, not believing what they had heard.

"What did you say Carla?" Namson asked, fear and pain coming with his question.

"Prateope, Castope's youngest daughter tried to attack the Realm. In the battle, Mike stopped a blast spell aimed at Heather and was killed. His body had landed on Heather and Prateope killed her as she lay pinned and defenseless!" Carla's thoughts were racked with her physical weeping. Namson looked to the others'. Tears of loss flowing down their cheeks. Glornina grabbed him desperately, sobbing, as the words of the deaths of her great grandfather and her grandmother came to her.

"Stay and clean this mess up, I will go and find out what has happened." Namson told them all. They could not even acknowledge his command for their weeping. Namson held Glornina and spelled them back to the Realm. There they found that Carla's words were indeed true. All Domains went to a time of mourning for their lost ones, for Mike and Heather were not the only losses that day or in the days that followed. Namson and Glornina sought out Charlesia and Mensalon and told them of the hero their son, Morsalon, had become, fighting alone against Castope.

CHAPTER SEVEN

The day after the battle in the Dark City, Namson placed Mike's body in the tomb with Gloreana, with these words; "As his father had brought the Plain and all those of it, to the power and greatness it was to be, Mike brought the Realm and all Domains to what they should and must be. I cannot replace him and I would not try. I only pray that I can see the future, the way of right, as he saw it."

Heather, after many debates, was laid to rest in the North East Domain. Tyrus had said that she should be with her parents, but the rest of the family had insisted that as his wife, she should be with him. Those who had been lost in the battles of the Dark City and the Realm, were given heroes funerals. There had been a few, so distraught over the loss of their loved ones and the loss of Mike and Heather, they simply gave up their lives and passed on to be with the loves they had lost. Tyrus had been one of those, for he followed his bride within a week of her burial. Sonilon placed his father's body in the tomb with his mother, that had been placed in a small grove in the back of the yard behind the castle. All those who could not bear the loss of their loved ones and joined them, were also given a heroes funeral.

———

Days after the funerals, Glornina was woke from her sleep by a voice that came to her mind. "Mistress of the Realm, I would speak with you," the voice told her. She lay next to Namson, listening to his breathing, waiting to see if he had woken as well. When sure he had not, she asked.

"Who is this?" her thoughts were calm, but her mind was racing.

"I am Cartope, oldest daughter of Castope and I ask for this time, that you and I can talk of stopping the wars," Glornina again checked her husband.

"I am listening Cartope," she told the voice.

"I and the those who have fled my mother with me, who have seen the wrong of the Dark Magic, have traveled to a far Domain. We will trouble you no more. Morsalon, my father, died helping me escape the evil and vile fate Castope, my mother, had plotted for me. I am tired of the killings. I am tired of the hatred. I am tired of the those who seek power for powers sake. I ask you now for peace between us," Cartope begged her. Glornina could not explain why she felt truth in the words Cartope had sent her, but she did.

"I would welcome peace," she told Cartope; "if it is truly meant," she kept her thoughts gentle.

"It is, it truly is," Cartope told her.

"Then it shall be peace," Glornina said.

"Thank you Mistress, thank you," The voice went silent. Glornina lay for the rest of the night, thinking of what she had heard. Not just the words, but the emotions she was sure were sent as well.

It was a month after the battles completion before Namson told of the taking of Castope. His tale went thusly;

"We were battling our way through the panicking horde that were trying to escape the Fortress, when we came to stairs. No one seemed to be left to come down them and we had not found Castope yet," he began his telling. "Some of her forces had managed to regroup, realizing who we were and tried to rally against us from the rear. The other ten turned and faced them as Glornina and I went up the stairs. When our sight cleared the top of the stairs, we could see two people. A man Glornina told me was Morsalon, and a woman, thirty feet beyond him, who had to be Castope. She was explaining to him the pain she was going to cause him before she would let him die. He must have tired of her talk, for he suddenly launched a blast spell at her. This surprised her and she barely got a shield up before it hit. That so enraged her she forgot all of her threats and hit him with a blast spell that blew him to pieces. Then she saw us on the stairs. She screamed curses at us and sent her spell. I shoved Glornina out of the way and matched her spell."

"Yeah you did," Glornina said and rubbed the side of her head. "I bounced off the wall!" This caused some to chuckle. Namson took her hand and smiled an apology at her. She returned his smile and accepted his hand. Namson returned to his telling.

"I don't think she realized that her powers were weakening until she saw the contact point of our spells coming closer. She made one final lunge, trying to drive her spell to me and then turned, dodged, and ran back down the hall, towards the burning. I chased after her and I saw her turn a corner."

"I couldn't believe he would just run off and leave me sitting there on the floor," Glornina stated, with a half grin at him. There were more chuckles from the listening group.

"As I neared the corner, I knew she would waiting for me to come around that corner. I stopped just before the corner and peeked around. I heard her voice scream to me from the dancing shadows created by the flames, "Come to me dead man," she had screamed and she threw a blast spell at me."

"I heard her as well," Glornina said with look of worry at Namson. "That's when I got off the floor and chased after him," she told all. There were many nodding heads. He smiled at her and turned back to the gathered.

"I dodged the spell and stepped around the corner. She stepped from the shadows and she was grinning. "You will die here," she screamed at me and again sent her spell at me, but she had no real power left. I met her spell and quickly over powered it. She seemed surprised when my spell hit her."

"That's when I got there and Namson's right," Glornina said as she moved closer to her husband. "There was a look of complete surprise on her face as she was consumed by the spell," she was almost whispering, as she looked to Namson, a sadness in her eyes. He again smiled at her and finished his telling.

"The fire was coming quickly and I knew we had to get out of there. I took Glornina's hand and we ran for the stairs. At the bottom, we found the others' waiting and they were alone, except for the remains of those who had tried to kill them. We all quickly retraced our steps to the rear door, and when we left the building, we found that all who had made it from the building, had been captured. We turned south and walked around the burning building and found all the commanders standing in front of the burning fortress, not doing anything, just standing there. I guess they were plotting a cook out or something." This brought laughter from all, especially those commanders.

"Mistress, a chill comes. Please return to the fire for warmth." Cartope turned her head and looked to Ralsanac. She smiled tiredly, nodded and turned her eyes back to the setting sun.

"Maybe one day, there will be no need for the wars, the pain, the deaths, Ralsanac." Her voice was very soft. The Dremlor looked to the one he loved with his very soul.

"If it is your will My Lady, it will be," was all he said. She turned to him. Her smile was pained and worried.

"It is my will Ralsanac, it is my will," she said softly and let him guide her back to the camp and the fire she hoped, would warm the dreaded chill that had been bred into her heart. He walked with her and a small smile came to his lips.

———※———

Somora had led his army away from the mountain that now separated them from the abating battle raging in the city. He wore a smile as he led them. They didn't stop until night had begun to fall. They found a camp site and small fires were started as they prepared an evening meal. When finished, he called his followers around him. He smiled at them and they all returned his smile. "We cannot live in the city for a time, for it will be watched, but I know of a place where we will be safe for now. Later, we can return and rebuild the city and then we can begin our planning to be the power that the magical Domains will fear, and one day, obey!" A quiet cheer came from them all. Somora turned and gathered Perilia and Dospora to him and they went to their shared bed.

Time continued its relentless march. Those of the age where life could not exist with them anymore, passed on. Children were born and grew to maturity in the Domains that had finally, found peace. All of the Domains began to feel the simple pleasure of contentment. As the years passed, new advancements came to all, especially the town of Zentler. Then, the fates decided that peace and contentment could not continue and added a new kind of threat to all.

CHARACTERS

HUMAN

<u>Beltyn</u>—magical powers, very high—youngest son of Megan—younger brother of Charlesia, Trayton-husband of Tylie—father of Gristamon—grandfather of Micky and Meligan

<u>Bill</u>—no magical powers—care taker of Canyon—husband of Kathy—father of Tom and Sandy—grandfather of Mike, Katie, Morgan, Megan, Marie, Willy, Candy

<u>Brandon</u>—magical powers, very high—son of Edgar and Suzie—younger brother of Chrystal-husband of Narisha—father of Jakelyn and Quoslon—grandfather of Taylor, Johnny, Xanaporia, Edward

<u>Brei</u>(Abrienne)—magical powers, very high—daughter of Jarpon and Katie—younger sister of Dana(Jardana)—wife of Crondasa—mother of Crodena, Xanalenor—great grandmother of Penny, Crandon, Xanaporia, Edward

Calene—no magical powers—wife of Sam—mother of Zack and Sally

Carla—magical powers, high, talker and seer-wife of Edward

Carmon—no magical powers—daughter of Porsia—wife of Tommy—mother of Bob and Marge

Charlesia—magical powers, high(shape changer)—daughter of Megan—older sister of Trayton and Beltyn—wife of Mensalon(elf)—mother of Morsalon and Belanor

Chrystal—magical powers, high—daughter of Edgar and Suzie—older sister of Brandon—wife of Trayton—mother of Ventia and Ralph—grandmother of Glornina, Prestilon, Edgar(young), Prelilian

Cindy—magical powers, high(talker)—daughter of Willy and Vicky—older sister of Cory(young)—wife of George—mother of Marklen and Peter—grandmother of Morgan(young), Darren, Croldena, Xanadera

Cory(old)—magical powers, high—Keeper of the Plain—son of Michael and Maria—older brother of DeeDee—husband of Sandy—father of Mike, Katie, Morgan, Megan—grandfather of Zachia, Heather, Talyus, Dana, Brei, Davian, Diasha, Charlesia, Trayton, Beltyne—great grandfather of Renoria, Zandian, Sonilon, Glory, Telador, Betsy

Cory(young)—magical powers, med—son of Willy and Vicky—younger brother of Cindy—husband of Felicia

Crandora-magical powers, high—son of Maelie and Crendosa—older brother of Xanadelis—husband of Renoria—father of Vandora and Pelinoria

Cranedoran—magical powers, high—King of Corsendora—husband of Xanaloren—father of Crendosa and Crondasa—grandfather of Crandora, Xanadelis, Crodena, Xanalenor

Crandora—magical powers, high—grandson of Cranedoran and Xanaloren—son of Crendosa and Maelie older brother of Xanadelis—husband of Renoria—father of Vandora and Pelinoria

Crendosa—magical powers, very high—prince of Corsendora—son of Cranedoran and Xanaloren—older brother of Crondasa—husband of Maelie—father of Crandora, Xanadelis—grandfather of Vandora, Pelinoria, Croldena, Xanadera

Croldena—Corsendorian general—magical powers, med—son of Xanadelis and Peter—grandson of Maelie and Crendosa—older brother of Xanadera

Crondasa—magical powers, very high—younger prince of Corsendora—son of Cranedoran and Xanaloren—younger brother of Crendosa—husband of Brei—father of Crodena, Xanalenor—grandfather of Penny, Crandon, Xanaporia, Edward

Dalyne—magical powers high—daughter of Jardan and Dana—older sister of Jardilan—wife of Renlon—mother of Dalynia and Norson

Dalynia—magical powers, high—granddaughter of Jardan and Dana—daughter of Dalyne and Renlon—older sister of Norson—wife of Micky

Dana(Jardana)—magical powers, high—daughter of Katie and Jarpon—older sister of Brie(Abrienne)-wife of Jardan—mother of Dalyne, Jardilan—great grandmother of Dalynia, Norson, Jarsolan, Jarsillia

Davian—magical powers, high—son of Morgan and Natoria—older brother of Diasha—husband of Jenny—father of Farsel, Paul—grandfather of Penny, Crandon, Morsley, Carla

DeeDee(Diedra)—magical powers, med—daughter of Michael and Maria—younger sister of Cory(old)—wife of Tom—mother of Marie, Willy, Candy—grandmother of Jardan, Narisha, Quansloe, Drayson, Cindy, Cory(young), Tommy, Jenny—great grandmother of Dalyne, Jardilan, Jakelyn, Quoslon, Polly, Selista, Renlon, Mary, Marklen, Peter, Fred, Paula, Bob(Robert), Marge, Farsel, Paul(young)

Dospora—magical powers, high(sorceress)—second mate of Somora

Drayson—magical powers, very high—daughter of Marie and Quensloe—younger sister of Jardan, Narisha-twin sister of Quansloe—wife of Matsar

<u>Dremlivar</u>—scholar of Contaria(scholars planet)—drawn into Willy when Willy spelled an end to a fire in Zentler—is part of Willy's consciousness—taught Maltakrine Dark Magic

<u>Edward</u>—Magical power, high—grandson of Marie and Quentloe—son of Quoslon and Xanalenor—younger brother of Xanaporia—husband of Carla

<u>Elamson</u>—magical powers, med—Leader of Calisonnos—husband of Ferlinos—father of Namson, Gerpinos

<u>Felicia</u>—magical powers, latent—daughter of J.R. and Christiana—younger sister of George—wife of Cory(young)—mother of Fred and Paula

<u>Ferlinos</u>—magical powers, med—Queen of Calisonnos—wife of Elamson—mother of Namson, Gerpinos

<u>Fred</u>—magical powers, med—son of Cory(young) and Felicia—older brother of Paula—husband of Sally

<u>George</u>—magical powers, low—son of J.R. and Christiana—older brother of Felicia—husband of Cindy—father of Marklen and Peter

<u>Gerpinos</u>—magical powers, very, very high—daughter of Elamson and Ferlinos—younger sister of Namson—wife of Vandora

Gloreana—magical powers, high (powerful seer)—wife of Mike—mother of Heather, Zachia(old), Talyus—grandmother of Renoria, Zandian, Sonilon, Glory, Telador, Betsy—great grandmother of Vandora, Pelinoria, Meladiana, Pentilian, Glornina, Prestilon, Morsley, Carla, Taylor, John Quentoria, Tarson

Glornina—magical powers, very, very high—daughter of Sonilon and Ventia—granddaughter of Heather and Tyrus—older sister of Prestilon—wife of Namson

Glory—magical powers, very high—granddaughter of Mike and Gloreana—daughter of Heather and Tyrus—younger sister of Sonilon—wife of Paul(young)—mother of Morsley and Carla

Gratimon—magical powers, high—Keeper of Magic of the North East Domain—husband of Wistoria—father of Tyrus, Maelie, Tylie—grandfather of Sonilon, Glory, Crandora, Xanadelis, Gristamon—great grandfather of Glornina, Prestilon, Morsley, Carla, Vandora, Pelinoria, Croldena, Xanadera, Micky, Meligan

Gristamon—magical powers, very high—grandson of Gratimon and Wistoria—son of Tylie and Beltyne husband of Polly—father of Micky and Meligan

Hannah—magical powers, very high—daughter of Prentiss and Kevin—younger sister of Sam—wife of Quansloe—mother of Polly and Selista—grandmother of Micky and Meligan

Heather—magical powers, very high(magic and seer)—daughter of Mike and Gloreana—twin sister of Zachia—older sister of Talyus—wife of Tyrus—mother of Sonilon, Glory—grandmother of Glornina, Prestilon, Morsley, Carla

Jakelyn—magical powers, high—daughter of Brandon and Narisha—older sister of Quoslon—wife of Telador—mother of Taylor and Johnny

Jardan—magical powers, high—son of Marie and Quasloe—older brother to Narisha, Quansloe, Drayson—father of Dalyne, Jardilan—grandfather of Dalynia, Norson, Jarsolan, Jarsillia

Jardilan—magical powers, high—son of Jardan and Dana—younger brother of Dalyne—husband of Marge father of Jarsalon and Jarsillia

Jarpon—magical powers, high—Keeper of Magic for Dolaris—husband of Katie—father of Dana and Brei—grandfather of Dalyne, Jardilan, Crodena, Xanalenor—great grandfather of Dalynia, Norson, Jarsolan, Jarsillia, Penny, Crandora, Xanaporia, Edward

Jarsolan—magical powers, very high—grandson of Jardan and Dana—son of Jardilan and Marge—older brother of Jarsillia-husband of Quentoria

Johnny—magical powers, high—grandson of Talyus and Maria(young)—son of Telador and

Katelyn—younger brother of Taylor—husband of Brandy

Kathy—no magical powers—wife of Bill—mother of Tom and Sandy—grandmother of Mike, Katie, Morgan, Megan, Marie, Willy, Candy

Katie—magical powers, very high—daughter of Cory(old)—twin sister of Mike—older sister of Morgan and Megan—wife of Jarpon—mother of Dana and Brei—grandmother of Dalyne, Jardilan, Crodena, Xanalenor—great grandmother of Dalynia, Norson, Jarsolan, Jarsillia, Penny, Crandora, Xanaporia, Edward

Kevin—latent magical powers, low—doctor of Zentler—husband of Prentiss—father of Sam and Hannah

Maelie—magical powers, very high—daughter of Gratimon and Wistoria—younger sister of Tyrus—older sister of Tylie—wife of Crendosa—mother of Crandora, Xanadelis—grandmother of Vandora, Pelinoria, Croldena, Xanadelis

Maldor—magical powers, low—husband of Renilis—father of Sen and Matsar—grandfather of Renoria, Zandian, Renlon, Mary—great grandfather of Vandora, Pelinoria, Meladiana, Pentilian, Dalynia, Norson

Marge—no magical powers—(Sensitive)—granddaughter of Candy and Paul—daughter of

Tommy and Carmon—wife of Jardilan—mother of Jarsolan and Jarsillia

Maria(old)—no magical powers—wife of Michael— mother of Cory(old) and DeeDee—grandmother of Mike, Katie, Morgan, Megan, Dana, Brei, Davian, Diasha, Charlesia, Trayton, Beltyne, Jardan, Narisha, Quansloe, Drayson, Cindy, Cory(young), Tommy, Jenny

Maria(young)—magical powers, high—daughter of Harry and Cretia—much younger sister of J.R.-wife of Talyus—mother of Telador and Betsy—grandmother of Taylor, Johnny, Quentoria, Tarson

Marie—magical powers, very high—daughter of Tom and DeeDee—older sister of Candy and Willy—wife of Quasloe, Quensloe—mother of Jardan, Narisha, Quasloe, Drayson—grandmother of Dalyne, Jardilan, Jakelyn, Quoslon, Polly, Selista, Renlon, Mary—great grandmother of Dalynia, Norson, Jarsolan, Jarsillia, Taylor, Johnny, Xanaporia, Edward, Micky, Meligan, Edgar(young), Prelilian, Meladiana, Pentilian

Marklen—magical powers, high—son of George and Cindy—older brother of Peter

Matsar—magical powers, very high—son of Renilis and Maldor—younger brother of Sen—husband of Drayson—father of Renlon and Mary—grandfather of Dalynia, Norson, Meladiana, Pentilian great grandfather of Danaliana, Karlten, Mistaria, Sertison, Creldora, Aaralyn, Jarsona, Paolaria

Megan—magical powers, med—daughter of Cory(old), Sandy—younger sister of Mike, Katie—twin sister of Morgan—never married—mother of Charlesia, Trayton, Beltyne—grandmother of Morsalon, Belanor, Ventia, Ralph, Gristamon—great grandmother of Cartope, Prateope, Penoria, Mentalon, Glornina, Prestilon, Edgar(young), Prelilian, Micky, Meligan

Meladiana—magical powers, very high—granddaughter of Zachia and Sen—daughter of Zandian and Mary—older sister of Pentilian—wife of Croldena

Meligan—magical powers, very high—granddaughter of Quansloe and Hannah—daughter of Gristamon and Polly—older sister of Edgar(young)

Michael—no magical powers—saved Valley from the creature who could not be named—saved Maria from the same creature-husband of Maria(old)—father of Cory(old) and DeeDee—grandfather of Mike, Katie, Morgan, Megan, Dana, Brei, Davian, Diasha, Charlesia, Trayton, Beltyne, Jardan, Narisha, Quansloe, Drayson, Cindy, Cory(young), Jenny

Micky—magical powers, very high—grandson of Quansloe and Hannah—son of Gristamon and Polly-older brother of Meligan

Mike—magical powers, ultimate—Overseer of the Realm-son of Cory(old), Sandy—twin brother of Katie-older brother of Morgan and Megan—husband of Gloreana—father of Heather, Zachia, Talyus—grandfather of Renoria, Zandian, Sonilon, Prestilon, Morsley, Carla, Telador, Betsy—great grandfather of Vandora, Pelinoria, Meladiana, Pentilian, Glornina, Prestilon, Morsley, Carla, Taylor, Johnny, Quentoria, Tarson

Morgan—magical powers, med—son of Cory(old) and Sandy—younger brother of Mike, Katie—twin brother of Megan—husband of Natoria—father of Davian, Diasha—grandfather of Farsel, Paul, Dinalaria, Brennon—great grandfather of Penny, Crandon, Morsley, Carla, Morgan(young), Darren, Quentoria, Tarson

Namson—magical powers, ultra high—Overseer of the Realm—son of Elamson and Ferlinos—husband of Glornina—father of Zachia(young), Glorian, Michele—grandfather of Mike[young], Mergania, Minsitoria, Heather, Telkor, Belkor, Mearlanor, Dafnorian, Ramnarson

Narisha—magical powers, very high—daughter of Marie and Quensloe—younger sister of Jardan—older sister of Quansloe and Drayson—wife of Brandon—mother of Jakelyn and Quoslon—grandmother of Taylor, Johnny, Xanaporia, Edward

Norson—magical powers, very high—grandson of Matsar and Drayson—son of Renlon and

Dalyne—younger brother of Dalynia—husband of Alice

Pelinoria—magical powers, very high—granddaughter of Zachia and Sen—daughter of Crandora and Renoria—younger sister of Vandora—wife of Morgan(young)

Pentilian—magical powers, very high—granddaughter of Zachia and Sen—daughter of Zandian and Mary-wife of Crandon

Perilia—magical powers, very high(Dremlor)—first mate of Somora

Porsia—no magical powers—house keeper for Willy and Vicky—mother of Carmon—grandmother of Bob and Marge

Prelilian—magical powers, very high—wife of Tarson

Pelinoria—magical powers, very high—granddaughter of Zachia and Sen—daughter of Crandora and Renoria—younger sister of Vandora

Pentilian—magical powers, very high—granddaughter of Zachia and Sen—daughter of Zandian and Mary—younger sister of Meladiana—wife of Crandon

Prentiss—no magical powers—younger sister of Paul—wife of Kevin—mother of Sam and Hannah

Prestilon—magical powers, very high—grandson of Trayton and Chrystal—son of Sonilon and Ventia-younger brother of Glornina—husband of Jarsillia

Quansloe—magical powers, very high—Keeper of the Plain—son of Marie and Quensloe—younger brother of Jardan, Narisha—twin brother of Drayson—husband of Hannah—father of Polly and Selista—grandfather of Micky, Meligan, Edgar, Prelilian—great grandfather of Danaliana, Karlten,

Quentloe—magical powers, low—husband of Marie—father of Quansloe and Drayson—step father of Jardan and Narisha

Quoslon—magical powers, high—grandson of Marie and Premton—son of Brandon and Narisha-younger brother of Jakelyn—husband of Xanalenor—father of Xanaporia and Edward

Renilis—magical powers, high—Keeper of Magic of the South East Domain—wife of Maldor—mother of Senfarna(Sen), Matsar(Mat)—grandmother of Renoria, Zandian, Renlon, Mary—great grandmother of Vandora, Pelinoria, Meladiana, Pentilian, Dalynia, Norson

Renlon-magical powers, very high—son of Matsar and Drayson—older brother of Mary—husband of Dalyne—father of Dalynia and Norson

Renoria—magical powers, very high—daughter of Zachia and Sen—older sister of Zandian—wife of Crandora—mother of Vandora and Pelinoria

Sam—magical powers, med—son of Kevin and Prentiss—older brother of Hannah—husband of Calene—father of Zack and Sally

Sandy—magical powers, med—daughter of Bill and Kathy—younger sister of Tom—wife of Cory(old)-mother of Mike, Katie, Morgan, Megan—grandmother of Zachia, Heather, Talyus, Dana, Brei, Davian, Diasha, Charlesia, Trayton, Beltyne—great grandmother of Renoria, Zandian, Sonilon, Glory, Farsel, Paul, Dinalaria, Brennon, Morsalon, Belanor, Ventia, Ralph, Micky, Meligan, Telador, Betsy, Dalyne, Jardilan, Crodena, Xanalenor,

Sen(Senfarna)—magical powers, very high—daughter of Renilis and Maldor—older sister of Matsar—wife of Zachia(old)—mother of Renoria, Zandian—grandmother of Vandora, Pelinoria, Meladiana, Pentilian

Somora—magical powers, very high(Dremlor)—King of those who escaped the battle of the Dark City

Sonilon—magical powers, very high—son of Tyrus and Heather—older brother of Glory—husband of Ventia—father of Glornina and Prestilon

Taylor—magical powers, very high—grandson of Brandon and Narisha—son of Jakelyn and

Telador—older brother of Johnny—husband of Mistian

Talyus—magical powers, very high—son of Mike and Gloreana—younger brother of Heather and Zachia-husband of Maria(young)—grandfather of Taylor and Johnny

Tarson—magical powers, high—general of Realm armies—grandson of Talyus and Maria—son of Brennon and Betsy—younger brother of Quentoria—husband of Prelilian

Tom—no magical power—son of Bill and Kathy—husband of DeeDee—father of Marie, Willy, Candy—grandfather of Jardan, Narisha, Drayson, Quansloe, Cindy, Cory(young), Tommy, Jenny—great grandfather of Dalyne, Jardilan, Jakelyn, Quoslon, Polly, Selista, Renlon, Mary, Marklen, Peter, Fred, Paula, Bob, Marge, Farsel, Paul

Tommy—no magical powers—very powerful seer and sensitive—son of Candy and Paul—older brother of Jenny—husband of Carmon—father of Bob and Marge

Trayton—magical powers, high(shape changer)—son of Megan—younger brother of Charlesia—older brother of Beltyn—husband of Chrystal—father of Ventia and Ralph—grandfather of Glornina, Prestilon, Edgar(young), Prelilian

Tylie—magical powers, very high—youngest daughter of Gratimon and Wistoria—younger sister of Tyrus and Maelie—wife of Beltyne—mother of Gristamon—grandmother of Micky and Meligan

Tyrus—magical powers, high—son of Gratimon and Wistoria—older brother of Maelie and Tylie—husband of Heather—father of Sonilon, Glory—grandfather of Glornina, Prestilon, Morsley, Carla

Vandora—Calisonnos General—magical powers, very high—husband of Gerpinos

Ventia—magical powers, very high—daughter of Trayton and Chrystal—wife of Sonilon—mother of Glornina and Prestilon

Vicky—no magical powers—daughter of Sam, the old town doctor—wife of Willy—mother of Cindy and Cory(young)

Willy—magical powers, low—Mayor of the town of Zentler—son of Tom and DeeDee—younger brother of Marie—twin brother of Candy—husband of Vicky—father of Cindy[young] and Cory(young)

Wistoria—magical powers, high—Keeper of Magic of the South West Domain—wife of Gratimon—mother of Tyrus, Maelie, Tylie—grandmother of Sonilon, Glory, Crandora, Xanadelis, Gristamon—great grandmother of Glornina, Prestilon, Morsley, Carla,

Vandora, Pelinoria, Croldena, Xanadera, Micky, Meligan

Xanalenor—magical powers, high—granddaughter of Cranedoran and Xanaloren—daughter of Crondasa and Brei—younger sister of Crodena—wife of Quoslon—mother of Xanaporia and Edward

Xanaloren—magical powers, high—Queen of Corsendora—wife of Cranedoran—mother of Crendosa and Crondasa—grandmother of Crandora, Xanadelis, Crodena, and Xanalenor

Xanaporia—magical powers, very high—Granddaughter of Crondasa and Brei—daughter of Quoslon and Xanalenor—older sister of Edward—wife of Gordon

Zachia—magical powers, very, very high—son of Mike and Gloreana—twin sister of Heather—older brother of Talyus—husband of Sen(Senfarna)—father of Renoria and Zandian—grandfather of Vandora, Pelinoria, Meladiana, Pentilian

Zack—magical powers, med—son of Kevin and Prentiss—older brother of Sally

Zandian—magical powers, high—son of Zachia and Sen—younger brother of Renoria—husband of Mary—father of Meladiana and Pentilian

VENTORIA

<u>Borack</u>—magical powers, med—Ruler of Bendine—husband of Borence—father of Dorack and Dorence

<u>Borence</u>—magical powers, low—wife of Borack—mother of Dorack and Dorence—grandmother of Semirack and Demerence

<u>Demerence</u>—magical powers, high—daughter of Simetor and Dorence—younger sister of Semirack

<u>Dorence</u>—magical powers, high—daughter of Borack and Borence—younger sister of Dorack—wife of Simetor—mother of Semirack and Demerence

<u>Dorsekor</u>—magical powers, med—daughter of Pilsekor and Ralitor—younger sister of Remitor

<u>Pelsikor</u>—magical powers, med—wife of Semitor—mother of Simetor, Pilsekor, Pielsakor—grandmother of Semirack, Demerence, Remitor, Dorsekor, and Minsikor

<u>Pielsakor</u>—magical powers, high(seer)—daughter of Semitor and Pelsikor—younger sister of Simetor and Pilsekor—wife of Roulitor—mother of Minsikor

<u>Pilsekor</u>—magical powers, high(talker)—daughter of Semitor and Pelsikor—younger sister of Simetor-older sister of Pielsakor—wife of Solitor and Ralitor—mother of Remitor(Solitor) and Dorsekor(Ralitor)

Ralitor—magical powers, med—friend of Solitor—second husband of Pilsekor—father of Dorsekor

Remitor—magical powers, high—son of Pilsekor and Solitor—older half brother of Dorsekor

Roulitor—magical powers, med—younger brother of Solitor—husband of Pielsakor—father of Minsikor

Semitor—friend of Mike—General, Ventorian army—husband of Pelsikor—father of Simetor, Pilsekor, Pielsakor—grandfather of Semirack, Demerence, Remitor, Dorsekor, Minsikor

Semotor—magical powers, high—great grandson of Pielsakor and Roulitor—leads Ventorian armies in battle of Dark City

Simetor—magical powers, high—son of Semitor and Pelsikor—older brother of Pilsekor and Pielsakor-husband of Dorence—father of Semirack and Demerence

ELVES

Belanor—magical powers, med—daughter of Charlesia and Mensalon—younger sister of Morsalon—wife of Bob

Mensalon—magical powers, med—son of Phemlon and Remlic—husband of Charlesia—father of Morsalon and Belanor

<u>Morsalon</u>—magical powers, high(Dark)—son of Charlesia and Mensalon—older brother of Belanor—mate of Castope—father of Cartope and Prateope

<u>Pelidora</u>—magical powers, med(healer)—healer of Overseer's palace

<u>Patoria</u>—magical powers, med—elder and most sensitive to Dark Magic

<u>Phemlon</u>—magical powers, med—leader of elves—husband of Remlic—father of Mensalon

OGRES

<u>Grable</u>—magical powers, med—mate of Minstoa—father of Meathoa

<u>Grames</u>—no magical powers—first mate of Grembo—twin sister of Grittle—mother of Gremble-grandmother of Manable and Minstoa—great grandmother of Morgable, Meathoa

<u>Graminel</u>—no magical powers—mate of Grastable—mother of Grandoa—grandmother of Manable and Minstoa—great grandmother of Morgable, Meathoa

<u>Grandoa</u>—magical powers, low—mate of Gremble—mother of Manable and Minstoa—grandmother of

Meathoa, Grimtal, Morgable—great grandmother of Gramable

Grastable—no magical powers—mate of Graminel—father of Grandoa—grandfather of Manable and Minstoa—great grandfather of Morgable, Meathoa, Grimtal—great, great grandfather of Gramable

Gratable—no magical powers—mate of Gromlee—father of Grimnoa—grandfather of Morgable

Gremble—no magical powers—leader of the ogres of the Realm—mate to Grandoa—father of Manable and Minstoa—grandfather of Morgable, Meathoa, Grimtal

Grembo—no magical power—leader of the Plains ogres—mate of Grames, Grittle—father of Gremble—grandfather of Manable and Minstoa—great grandfather of Morgable, Meathoa

Griliana—magical powers, high—daughter of Grisble and Marthoa

Grimnoa—magical powers, low—daughter of Gratable and Gromlee—mate of Manable—mother of Morgable

Grisble—no magical powers—leader of ogres on Calisonnos—mate of Marthoa—father of Griliana

Grittle—no magical powers—second mate of Grembo—twin sister of Grames—half mother of Gremble

Gromlee—no magical powers—mate of Gratable—mother of Grimnoa—grandmother of Morgable

Manable—magical powers, med—son of Gremble and Grandoa—mate of Grimnoa—father of Morgable

Marthoa—magical powers, low—mate of Grisble—mother of Griliana—grandmother of Gramable

Meathoa—magical powers, high—granddaughter of Gremble, Grandoa,—daughter of Grable and Grimnoa

Minstoa—magical powers, med—daughter of Gremble and Grandoa—mate of Grable—mother of Meathoa

Morgable—magical powers, high—great grandson of Grembo, Grames, Grastable, Graminel—grandson of Gremble, Grames, Gratable, Gromlee—son of Manable and Grimnoa

DRAGONS

Cartile—magical powers, low—leader of dragons of the Realm—mate of Jastile-father of Chartile and Semitile

<u>Chartile</u>—magical powers. low—son of Cartile and Jastile—killed by Cartile when he tried to take command of the dragons of the Realm

<u>Hanatile</u>—magical powers, low—mate of Nalatile

<u>Jastile</u>—magical powers, low—mate of Cartile—mother of Chartile and Semitile

<u>Merlintile</u>—magical powers, very high—son of Crastamor and Crelintile—mate of Semitile

<u>Nalatile</u>—magical powers, low—mate of Hanatile

<u>Semitile</u>—magical powers, med—daughter of Cartile and Jastile—mate of Merlintile

<u>Welerlintile</u>—magical powers, low—ex mate of Chartile

FAIRY FOLK

<u>Alasteen</u>—magical powers, high—queen of the fairy folk of the Plain—mate of Rarteen

<u>Rarteen</u>—magical powers, med—mate of Alasteen

<u>Sanlear</u>—magical powers, high-Queen fairy of the Valley—mate of Tanlear

Tanlear—magical powers, med—mate of Sanlear

Tremliteen—magical powers, med—messenger for Namson

UNICORNS

Dereress—magical powers, med—lead stallion of Plains unicorns—mate of Peantine

Peantine—magical powers, med—mate of Dereress

Persetine—magical powers, med—twin sister of Wersetine—mate of Renless

Ranline—magical powers, med—friend of Renless— mate of Wersetine

Renless—magical powers, med—lead stallion of Valley unicorns—mate of Persetine

Wersetine—magical powers, med—mate of Ranline

WOLVES

Grrale—no magical powers—leader of Realm pack

Terryle—no magical powers—mate of Grrale

TROLLS
(some have magical powers)
(Y—yes N—no)

<u>Coursel</u>-(y)—med—leader of the young trolls of the Plain

<u>Morsel</u>-(y)—low-leader of the young trolls of the Valley

<u>Morson</u>-(n)—mate of Worsel

<u>Mursel</u>-(n)—leader of the Plains troll clan

<u>Ponsel</u>-(y)—high-leader of the young trolls of the Realm

<u>Porsel</u>-(n)—second in command of trolls in the Realm

<u>Worsel</u>-(n)—leader of the Valley troll clan

<u>Zardan</u>-(n)—leader of the troll clan of the Realm

EAGLES

<u>Kraslar</u>—no magical powers—old King of the Plains Eagles

<u>Marlar</u>—no magical powers—mate of Ralitan—King of the Plains Eagles

<u>Nilitan</u>—no magical powers—mate of Vralar—Queen of the Realms Eagles

Ralitan—no magical powers—mate of Marlar—Queen of the Plains Eagles

Vralar—no magical powers—mate of Nilitan—King of the Realms Eagles

BELTHUME

Besonlor—magical powers, med—strongest talker of Belthume

Bursanlac—[dragon]-magical powers, low—Leader of the Black Dragons

Delakas—magical powers, med—Leader of the Black Dragon Riders

Kailen—magical powers, low—First Lieutenant of Ransidar—husband of Mistilane

Martoran—magical powers, high—King of Belthume—husband of Restone

Ransidar—magical powers, low—General of Belthume's armies

Restone—magical powers, high—Queen of Belthume—wife of Martoran

DARK CITY

<u>Balakrine</u>-magical powers, high—son of Saltakrine—
father of Castope

<u>Cartope</u>—magical powers, high—oldest daughter of
Castope—older sister of Prateope

<u>Castope</u>—magical powers, high—Ruler of Dark
City—daughter of Balakrine—granddaughter of
Saltakrine-mother of Dremlon, Cartope, Prateope

<u>Dremlon</u>—magical powers, high—son of Castope and a
demon—father of all Dremlors

<u>Prateope</u>-magical powers, high—youngest daughter of
Castope and Morsalon—younger sister of Cartope

<u>Ralsanac</u>—magical powers, high—Dremlor advisor to
Castope—loves and saves Cartope

<u>Ragella</u>—magical powers, high—sorceress(seer, talker)

<u>Saltakrine</u>-magical powers, high—son of Palakrine—fa-
ther of Balakrine—grandfather of Castope—founder
of Dark City

<u>Somora</u>—magical powers, high—Dremlor—leader of
those escaping Castope's command—mate of Perilia
and Dospora

<u>Starle</u>—magical powers, high—son of demon and
sorceress